PUFFIN BOOKS

RUNNING
FOR GOLD

Owen Slot is chief sports reporter on *The Times*. He has three times been named Sports Feature Writer of the Year and three times Sports News Reporter of the Year.

Books by Owen Slot

Running for Gold
Cycling for Gold

RUNNING
FOR GOLD

★ ★ ★ ★ ★ ★ ★ ★ ★ ★ ★ ★ ★ ★

OWEN SLOT

PUFFIN

PUFFIN BOOKS

Published by the Penguin Group
Penguin Books Ltd, 80 Strand, London WC2R ORL, England
Penguin Group (USA) Inc., 375 Hudson Street, New York, New York 10014, USA
Penguin Group (Canada), 90 Eglinton Avenue East, Suite 700, Toronto, Ontario, Canada M4P 2Y3
(a division of Pearson Penguin Canada Inc.)
Penguin Ireland, 25 St Stephen's Green, Dublin 2, Ireland (a division of Penguin Books Ltd)
Penguin Group (Australia), 250 Camberwell Road, Camberwell, Victoria 3124, Australia
(a division of Pearson Australia Group Pty Ltd)
Penguin Books India Pvt Ltd, 11 Community Centre, Panchsheel Park, New Delhi – 110 017, India
Penguin Group (NZ), 67 Apollo Drive, Rosedale, Auckland 0632, New Zealand
(a division of Pearson New Zealand Ltd)
Penguin Books (South Africa) (Pty) Ltd, Block D, Rosebank Office Park, 181 Jan Smuts Avenue, Parktown
North, Gauteng 2193, South Africa

Penguin Books Ltd, Registered Offices: 80 Strand, London WC2R ORL, England

puffinbooks.com

First published 2012
001 – 10 9 8 7 6 5 4 3 2 1

Text copyright © Owen Slot, 2012
All rights reserved

The moral right of the author has been asserted

Set in Baskerville MT Std 13/16 pt
Typeset by Palimpsest Book Production Limited, Falkirk, Stirlingshire
Made and printed in Great Britain by Clays Ltd, St Ives plc

British Library Cataloguing in Publication Data
A CIP catalogue record for this book is available from the British Library

ISBN: 978-0-141-33217-8

www.greenpenguin.co.uk

MIX
Paper from
responsible sources
FSC
www.fsc.org   FSC™ C018179

Penguin Books is committed to a sustainable
future for our business, our readers and our planet.
This book is made from Forest Stewardship
Council™ certified paper.

ALWAYS LEARNING   **PEARSON**

For Ivo, Maddie and Oliver

CONTENTS

★ 1 ★

DANNY POWELL

Until 20 May, no one had taken Danny Powell very seriously. They liked him and they kind of guessed that he was extra special because they all knew he could run so blisteringly fast. Wow, could he run fast! Everyone knew he had the quickest pair of feet in the school. In fact, they all knew that Danny could run faster than anyone in any school in the whole of the United Kingdom.

Every summer it seemed, Danny would go to the UK School Games and come back champion. Whenever those UK School Games came round, the following Monday morning you almost knew that your school email inbox at Newham Secondary would deliver the same news: that Danny Powell had won the 100 metres. Again. This meant that he was the best young sprinter in the country. Still. Indeed, pretty much everyone who had ever met Danny knew that, one day, he would be a professional athlete.

But where the whole Danny story got a bit ridiculous

was when he told them that in the summer holidays after his A levels, he was going to beat Usain Bolt.

Oh, yeah, Danny? No one beats Usain Bolt. Usain Bolt is the fastest human being of all time. Dream on, Danny.

Danny hated the idea of being a show-off and so he had not intended to let it slip. He loved to run and he loved to win. It was, by far, the best thing in his life. But he never bragged. Not around school. Nowhere. He never wanted other people to think that he was a show-off, a swank. And so his dream of beating Bolt was one that he kept completely to himself. And if it wasn't for a robbery, from right under his nose, then it would have remained there.

It happened one day during school lunchtime. He wished it hadn't. And it was the stupid thief's fault. Such a stupid, dozy, hopeless thief. Danny was hanging around the school gates, the place he and his mate, loudmouth Anthuan, and a bunch of their mates in the sixth form always hung out at lunchtime.

No one saw the thief coming. He was probably only twenty years old, average in height and average in looks. He wore dark jeans and a dark T-shirt, but they only realized all that afterwards. At the time, all anyone realized was that with one slightly nervous and aggressive sweep of his arm, he had ripped off the shoulder bag that Jess had hanging loosely from her shoulder. He did it with such force that Jess, yelping in shock more than pain, fell to the ground.

Danny knew that it was wrong to get involved. *Keep your nose out of trouble.* That's what his father always told him. So he stood and, for about two seconds, he watched as the bloke hotfooted it down the pavement. A series of thoughts flashed through Danny's mind: *Should I let him go? Should I stay out of trouble? Might I get hurt? And should I stay here and look after Jess?* And then, in that very split second that he had persuaded himself to be cautious and avoid trouble, the thief stopped running and turned, and it seemed that he was smiling. He may just have been panting, out of breath, but from where Danny was standing it seemed that he had a triumphant grin on his face. And that was that. Danny was off.

The sight of Danny Powell at full speed is astonishing. He has a long stride and a natural balance, which combine into a beautiful elegance. So, when he is sprinting, it doesn't look as though he is trying hard – it hardly seems as though his feet touch the ground; it is more as if he is gliding. But, boy, does he move fast.

He flashed like lightning down the road. It was about two seconds before the thief turned again and realized that he was being pursued and, at that stage, his smile disappeared for good. Danny started closing on him quick and as the distance between them was rapidly disappearing, passers-by moved out of the way and stopped and stared. As Danny got even nearer, the difference between his speed and the thief's was so great, it was almost funny. The thief's arms were pumping hard, flailing desperately from side to side but, compared to Danny, he was going so slowly it was like he was running in treacle.

Danny got closer and closer: thirty metres away, twenty-five metres, twenty . . . Suddenly, he was almost able to touch him when the thief turned round, saw that he was beaten and dropped the bag.

And that was when Danny stopped running. He didn't want to catch the thief. What would he have done to him? Fought him? He had never fought anyone; he wouldn't know what to do.

So he just stopped running and picked up Jess's bag. And that was that. End of episode. At least so he thought.

The next day at Newham Secondary, they had school assembly. School assembly was held every Thursday and it was usually pretty dull. During school assembly, Danny and Anthuan and most of their friends would have their mobile phones out and would be busy texting each other. If you got caught with your mobile phone during assembly, it would be confiscated for the rest of the day. But hardly anyone ever got caught, at least not Danny or Anthuan; they were far too smart for that.

Up on the school stage stood the headmaster, Mr McCaffrey. As teachers go, Mr McCaffrey was OK. But he loved the sound of his own voice – and so he loved Thursdays and school assembly because that was his chance to be centre stage and do lots of talking. Mr McCaffrey also had a greying goatee beard that he seemed rather fond of even if he was slightly too old for it. He would stand and talk and stroke his goatee at the same time. Danny often wondered if Mr McCaffrey had any idea that barely anyone ever listened to a word he said.

Danny scrolled down the inbox of his phone. He was hoping for a text from Ricky, his brother. He adored Ricky, but Ricky was a student, away at university, and he never got in touch. Danny hated that. He missed Ricky. But he thought he might get a text from him today.

It was then, suddenly, that Danny's attention to his phone was ripped away. Anthuan gave him a hefty nudge in the ribs with his elbow. 'Dan,' he whispered, out of the side of his mouth. 'Listen up, Dan, he's talking about you.'

Anthuan was right. Up on stage, Mr McCaffrey was babbling on, as ever, but he was now babbling on about a robbery incident the previous day. *Oh no, please no!* thought Danny. He hated the idea of being the centre of attention.

'. . . and this thief thought he had got away with it,' was what Mr McCaffrey was saying, 'but he hadn't accounted for the fact that at Newham Secondary, we happen to have the fastest young schoolboy in the country. So well done, Danny Powell.'

Mr McCaffrey then started clapping and there was a flutter of applause around the school hall. Danny looked down, trying to avoid everyone's stares. But then Mr McCaffrey carried on: 'And so I would like to ask Danny Powell to come up here for a minute.'

Oh no! You can't be serious! thought Danny. But the headmaster was. And it was on stage that the day really took a turn for the worse.

'Danny,' Mr McCaffrey said, turning to him, 'well done. You have made us all proud.'

'Thank you, sir,' Danny replied.

'And here we are, at the start of the athletics season. Have you got any big plans?'

Danny felt flustered. *What should I say?* he thought. So he decided he may as well be honest – and he just said: 'Yes.'

'Would you fancy running in the Olympics?' Mr McCaffrey asked.

'Of course,' Danny replied. 'Who wouldn't?'

'Exactly,' said Mr McCaffrey. 'Good luck, Danny.' And Danny had just started walking off the stage when Mr McCaffrey said: 'One other thing, Danny . . .' So Danny stopped. '. . . I don't suppose you could beat Usain Bolt, could you?'

Danny paused. *What should I say? What should I say?* And before he could stop himself, he told the truth. 'It's going to be tough, but that's certainly the plan, sir.'

The second that Danny had let that sentence fly from his mouth, he wanted to catch it and take it back again. The school hall erupted with squeals and whistles and quite a lot of laughter. And Danny couldn't stand people laughing at him.

Five minutes later, when assembly was over, the school hall had emptied and the students had piled out into the open air, he was made to feel even worse. 'Dream on, Danny!' was the first comment that was flung his way. 'Danny, I hear Usain Bolt's really scared.' 'Danny, Bolt could beat you on one leg.' And: 'Danny, what planet are you on? Come back down to earth, you might enjoy it down here.'

Ha! Ha! Very funny, the lot of you, thought Danny as he turned left out of the school hall towards the classrooms. He hated people thinking he was arrogant. But what he hated the most was the idea that people didn't believe in him, that they should laugh at the very idea that he was going to beat Usain Bolt. *I'll prove them all wrong*, he said to himself. 'Bolt could beat you on one leg,' they said. How he wanted to ram those comments down their precious little throats.

For the rest of the day, Danny was not allowed to forget it. Most people were too scared to say anything, but he could see them smirking to each other.

Some were brave enough to comment. 'Usain's got no chance!' was one sarcastic comment. He hated that.

'Good luck against Bolt!' were the words of one younger boy. And he probably meant it, but Danny didn't like that either.

At the end of the school day, feeling thoroughly dispirited, Dan sought out the company of Anthuan. But that didn't turn out to be a very good idea either.

'Are you coming out to the movies tomorrow night, Dan?' he asked.

'I can't,' Danny replied. 'I've got to train, haven't I?'

'We're *all* going,' Anthuan said, slightly pleadingly, as if trying to play on Danny's conscience.

'I just can't,' Danny replied, shrugging. 'You know that. Training. I've got to train. I've *always* got to train.'

Anthuan seemed disappointed and went quiet. They walked out of the school gates together. And then Anthuan asked him a question that really surprised him. And the way he asked it suggested that he was slightly uncomfortable about it himself.

'Dan,' he said, 'do you really think you could beat Usain Bolt?'

Danny stopped walking, paused for a second and then answered: 'Ant, I know it sounds crazy, and I know I sound stupid when I say it. But this is my dream. The Olympics are coming. I've got a one in a million chance of beating that guy. So yes, I do think I have a chance. It's a slim one, but it's still a chance. What do you think?'

Anthuan looked down at the ground and furrowed his brow as if he was thinking seriously. 'I think you're my best mate in the world, Dan,' he replied slowly. 'And I don't want to be hard on you. But I hate seeing people laugh at you like they did today, you know that. So come on, Dan. You're so young still and maybe you should remember that. You could be out having fun tomorrow night, but you don't want to. Do you really think you're ready to race Bolt? I just can't help feeling that if you raced Bolt now, he'd have time to finish the race and eat a cheese sandwich before you came through the line.'

Dan looked at Anthuan with disgust. He felt angry and let down. 'Oh, right, I see. So not even my best mate believes in me. See ya.' And with that, he trotted off down the road and jumped straight on the 215 bus, leaving Anthuan standing alone.

Danny was furious. But, more than that, he was really upset. *Not even Ant believes in me*, he thought to himself. *I'll just have to prove him wrong too.*

★ 2 ★

THE OLYMPICS

If you are an athlete like Danny, then you have one dream, one massive dream that spills from side to side in your head like water in a glass. It washes over you and it never washes out; it dominates your thoughts and it gets in the way of the rest of your life. It can be a disaster for your schoolwork because it makes it so hard to concentrate on anything else. The Olympics. You spend every spare second of your life dreaming about the Olympics.

Sometimes Danny's dad, Roy, would catch Danny daydreaming and he knew instinctively what Danny was thinking about. 'Get on with your studies, my boy,' he would say. 'Forget the Olympics.'

'Don't know what you're talking about!' Danny would reply. But he was lying and he knew his father knew he was lying and so he would smile cheekily too.

It was impossible to forget about the Olympics. How could you forget about the Olympics when they were right here on your doorstep?

The summer Olympics were only two and a half months away. The London Olympics. London 2012. The greatest show on earth. That was what they sometimes called the Olympic Games. 'The greatest show on earth.' And here they were, the Olympics, in his very own city.

But the Olympics were not only in Danny's very own city, they were in his very own neighbourhood. Danny lived in east London, in a neighbourhood called Stratford. And the Olympics? They were heading for Stratford too. The Olympic Stadium, the very stadium where Bolt would be running, was barely three kilometres from Danny's house.

In fact, Danny had lived with the whole project from beginning to end. Every school day for the last four years, he would turn left out of his house in Widdin Street and head 200 metres to Anthuan's house, and together they would walk to Newham Secondary, taking a short detour via Bridge Road where they would witness first-hand the Olympics coming to life.

Bridge Road was on the edge of what seemed like a monstrously large building site. This was the huge plot of land that would be built into the Olympic Park. In Danny's mind, the Olympic Park was going to be the biggest playground in the world: it would have athletics, swimming, hockey, cycling, basketball. You name it, pretty much the entire Olympic Games was going to happen here.

At first, Danny and Anthuan could see nothing from Bridge Road because the entire building project was going on behind a high, blue fence. All they could tell was that the building site made a deafening noise and threw a haze of dust up into the air. But, around three years ago, things started to change. One day, when they were walking to school, they got their first glimpse of one of the new buildings, covered in scaffolding, poking its head above the fence, as if it was finally saying hello to the world. And this building simply got taller and taller, and as it neared completion, it became increasingly obvious that this was the main Olympic Stadium, the stadium for athletics, the stadium where Usain Bolt would run.

'Imagine Usain in that place,' Danny and Anthuan would say to each other, laughing. They could not believe their luck: that this was all going to take place here. And soon they had renamed the Olympic Stadium 'Bolt's Second Home'.

But it wasn't just Bolt's Second Home they could see. If they took another route, which afforded a better view into the park, they could see a whole team of buildings all slowly rising out of the ground until they were huge, gleaming, beautiful. And they were so close you could almost touch them. The aquatic centre, which was where the Olympic swimming and diving would take place, looked really cool; it had a strange, undulating roof that was designed to make it look like a stingray. And then there was the velodrome for the cyclists, the arena for basketball and a whole lot more. With some of the buildings, the boys had no clue what sport would be taking place there. But no matter, it was just so tantalizing to imagine the best athletes on the planet all coming here, right to their doorstep.

And to think that Danny's dad expected him to forget about the Olympics! Danny knew his A levels were important. But he also had a feeling, as if it was something in his blood and in his bones, that the Olympics were important too. Danny felt drawn to that Olympic Park, as if he was caught by some kind of magnetic force. Sometimes, when he was on his own on the way back from school, he would stand and stare at the park and allow himself to drift off in a long Olympic daydream.

But Danny's dad could hardly pretend that the Olympics weren't important. Danny's dad loved the Olympics. Every four years when the Olympic Games came round, he always made the entire family sit round the TV and watch it. First and foremost, they would watch the athletics, but they seemed to watch absolutely everything: the swimming, the gymnastics, the boxing, the judo, the wrestling, the taekwondo – all these weird different forms of fighting that seemed to be banned in the house but for which you could win medals at the Olympics!

Danny's mother loved the gymnastics. Danny's

father loved cheering on the Africans in the long-distance running events. Danny's older brother, Ricky, pretended that he wasn't interested, but, whenever the weightlifting was on, he would sit there watching, absolutely entranced, cheering on the big men from Russia and Bulgaria. No one quite understood why he suddenly became Russian or Bulgarian over the period of the Olympics, but there was no talking him out of it!

And Danny? For him it was simple. His first memory of the Olympics was when he was six, although he could remember them four years later and four years after that too. But he had a very specific recollection of one specific moment in each of the Olympics that he had seen. It was as if he had a special place in his mind for storing away the memories of one race, one race every four years: the men's 100 metres, the race to be the fastest man on earth.

And that was why he felt he already knew Usain Bolt. He had never met Bolt, never even seen him in the flesh, but, when he watched Bolt win the Olympics in Beijing four years earlier, he had been absolutely entranced. He had recorded the race on the TV and he must have watched it a hundred times since. More like a thousand times. He was mesmerized by Bolt's long stride and by the speed with which his feet left the ground. And he could not believe that Bolt was so much better in Beijing than everyone else, so much better that he had started celebrating his victory long before he had even got to the finishing line.

The night that Bolt had won the 100 metres in Beijing, Danny had found it hard to sleep. He kept on replaying the race over and over in his mind. At two o'clock in the morning, when he had pretty much given up trying to sleep, he had sneaked downstairs, switched on the TV and watched the race again. He watched it in slow motion; he watched it fast; he watched it with the sound turned down and with the sound turned up.

How did Bolt do it? That was the question rattling through Danny's mind.

But really there were other questions that he wanted answering: *Could I do it too? Could I come to the Olympics, when they are in London, and run that fast too? Would it be possible, here in London, for me to beat Usain Bolt?*

★ 3 ★

STEVE THE SPIKE

Danny stepped off the 215 bus, turned off the road, into the car park and towards the broad building ahead. This was his training facility, the place where his dream was allowed to grow. In school, they could laugh at his dream, but here is where it was nurtured. This is where it seemed real.

Danny had a regimented life: he would get up in the morning and go to school; after school he would go to training, then back home, supper, homework and bed; school, training, home, home-work, bed. Over and over again: school, training, home, homework, bed, pretty much every single day. If you want to be Olympic champion, you have no alternative, at least that is what Steve the Spike told him.

And Danny liked listening to Steve. Steve was possibly both the smartest and the meanest coach in the world. Maybe the best coach in the world too. But he was probably the only person on the planet who really believed in him. Danny was eighteen; he was still at school, he hadn't even taken his driving test, and yet Steve completely and utterly believed that Danny could win the Olympics.

So he believed and trusted Steve. It didn't help having Anthuan telling him the opposite: don't train, don't go home to bed, come out to the movies with your mates. There were so many times that Danny wanted to do exactly what Anthuan told him. He wanted to go out with Ant and the others; he knew how much fun they had and he wanted that for himself too.

But he had a dream, and he was determined to follow it. And he knew that was more important.

When Danny arrived at the Lee Valley Stadium to train, he also knew he had to clear out of his head everything that was supposed to be inside his head at school: A levels, history, business studies, sports science and all the rest of it. He had to turn off one switch and flick on another. Turn off school and turn on running. Running fast. Every single second of his time down here at Lee Valley had to be devoted to that one single goal: training his legs to get from the start of a 100-metres race to the finish line as quickly as they possibly could.

Steve the Spike called their training centre 'The home of speed'.

'Feel the need for speed, Danny!' he would say. And almost every day his greeting to Danny would be, 'Hello, Speedboy.' That was his nickname for

Danny, Speedboy, and Danny liked it. 'Hello, Speedboy,' Steve would say, 'you brought your speed today?'

But today, as Danny pushed open the door into the stadium, he knew he wasn't in the right frame of mind. He mumbled a 'Hello' to Gladys, the nice lady who worked on the reception desk, but he was distracted. He wasn't thinking about speed. In fact, he had probably left his speed behind. He was thinking instead about Ant and what he had said about Usain Bolt and the cheese sandwich. And he could feel a deep sense of anger within himself. Ant had said that Usain Bolt could finish the race and eat a cheese sandwich before Danny came through the line!

The cheek of it, he thought to himself. But he hated the fact that this was making him cross. *How can Ant and a cheese sandwich make me so angry?*

'Hey, Speedboy!' Danny heard Steve's voice almost the second he walked through the door. It was loud and excessively enthusiastic. 'There are now seventy-one days to the Games. Are you ready to train hard?'

Danny rolled his eyes. 'Yeah, Spike,' he said unconvincingly. Steve the Spike was like a walking countdown clock; every single day that Danny came to training, Steve would tell him how long to go until the Olympics.

'Good!' barked Steve. 'Get changed, and then I

want to see you down in my office in five minutes. We've got plans to make. And then I'm going to kill you.'

Steve the Spike always seemed to have two things on his mind.

One: he always wanted to kill Danny. Every day, he said, he wanted Danny to die. Danny knew what he meant: he wanted to train Danny so hard that Danny's whole body would ache because of the pain and Steve wanted the pain to be so bad that Danny couldn't run any more, so bad in fact that he felt he was about to die. That, for Steve the Spike, was the definition of death. He wanted Danny to die, and then to rise again from the dead – a bit like Jesus, Danny thought, except he was pretty confident he could have beaten Jesus over 100 metres. But Steve wanted Danny to die and rise again every day, today, tomorrow and then the day after that. That was another thing that Spike liked to bark at Danny every day: 'Yo, Speedboy! You ready to die today?'

Two: planning. Steve loved to make plans. But the important bit was this: they were always good plans. Genius plans for becoming the fastest man in the world. That was why Danny was able to put up with Steve the Spike forever trying to kill him.

The point about Steve was that you had to understand his background; you had to know what he had gone through and where his nickname had come from. Back in the 1970s, Steve had been one of the fastest young kids in the country, one of the fastest young kids in the world. In fact, Steve then was pretty much like Danny now. And, like Danny, Steve had one dream, and that was to be the Olympic 100-metres champion.

But Steve's dream had come crashing down around him and was broken in the worst way imaginable. In 1982, Steve was selected for the British senior team for the first time ever, to run in the European Championships in Athens. This was a great moment for him: to represent his country on the athletics track made him feel so proud. It felt like the greatest day of his life, and yet he was only twenty-one and people who knew anything about running would say to each other: 'This boy has got a great future ahead of him.' What they thought was that Steve would run in Athens and probably do *quite* well, but they thought that two years later, when he was older and more experienced, he would go to his first Olympics and probably do *really, really* well.

But Steve never talked to Danny about Athens. He never discussed what happened there. Danny knew why. Everyone knew.

Steve got to the final of the 100 metres in Athens. He had done brilliantly to reach that stage, but he didn't leave it at that. In the final, he ran the race of his life and won the bronze medal. Not bad for a twenty-one-year-old. And there were stories in the newspapers with headlines like 'Steve sprints to medal triumph', 'Britain's new speed machine' and 'Britain's boy wonder'.

Four days later though came the accident that would end it all for him, a horrible, bloody, freak accident that no one had ever seen on the track before. It was the relay race and Steve was the second to run for the British team. When he was handing over the baton to the third British runner, he had got Great Britain into first place, but his mistake was that, having handed over the baton, he fell over. He was so exhausted from the effort that he just crashed to the ground. It was a stupid thing to have done and that is one of the many reasons why Steve hardly ever spoke a word about it to anyone.

Because, as Steve crashed to the ground, he fell in front of the Italian runner next to him. Giovanni Bongiorni was the Italian man's name. Steve had never forgotten it. Bongiorni was running at full pelt and had not had the chance to check his stride. He had probably not even seen Steve's right leg on the ground in his very path. And Bongiorni's left foot had come down on the back of Steve's leg and the spikes in Bongiorni's shoe tore a great gash down Steve's calf and into his Achilles tendon.

And that was the end of Steve's running career. And that was also why Steve was now so intense, why he cared so much, why he was so stressed sometimes, why he shouted, why he wanted Danny to die every day on the track. Because he did not want Danny to miss out on the very opportunity that should have been his.

After Steve's leg had been gashed on the track in Athens, he was treated at the side of the track by a British team doctor who gave him an injection to dull the pain and recommended that he be taken away to hospital, straight away. Steve was carried away on a stretcher, but, as he went, he had seen the doctor shaking his head slowly, with a dark look on his face.

The problem for Steve, as he would learn over the next week in hospital, is that the Achilles tendon is about the most important piece of kit that a runner needs. The Achilles transfers power and strength and information from the muscles in your leg to your feet and back again. Basically, if your Achilles isn't working, then you are not going to be much of a runner.

And that was why Steve never ran competitively again. The doctors never made his Achilles completely better. They tried, but Steve found that whenever he trained hard, the pain would come back, and when the pain came back, he could never find quite the same speed. And so he trained harder and harder, desperate to overcome the problem, but the harder he trained, the fiercer the pain, and the fiercer the pain, the harder it was for him to hit the same phenomenal speeds that once made him one of the fastest kids in the world.

It got to the stage where Steve would die in training every day. He would run himself so hard his whole body ached and his Achilles seemed to cry out to him: 'Stop! Please stop!' And so Steve would limp off the track, and then he would limp home, and then he would find that he was limping the next day too. In fact, Steve soon realized that he was going to limp for the rest of his life. And you can't hope to be the fastest sprinter in the world if you have a limp. So, for Steve, that was the end. He quit the sport. His dream was over.

And that was how Steve got his nickname, Steve the Spike. Or just Spike for short. To Danny, it seemed like a bad joke, but everyone seemed to call him that.

And that was also why Steve the Spike cared so much about Danny. He knew what Danny had put into his life as a runner. He knew the sacrifices that Danny was making. He knew that eighteen-year-old boys wanted to go out, hang out with their friends, go to the movies. And he knew that Danny almost always managed to say no. So it wasn't just that he liked Danny, he also admired him. And he wanted

Danny to achieve what he himself had never managed. He wanted it so desperately for him. And so pretty much every day, he went out with the intention of killing Danny on the track.

★ 4 ★

HOW TO BEAT USAIN BOLT, PART 1

Spike scratched the back of his head impatiently. He studied Danny. Danny had just walked into his office and he didn't look right. Spike knew from the look on his face that Danny hadn't brought his 'Speed-head' with him.

So he asked Danny what was up and Danny told Spike about school and the cheese sandwich and Spike laughed. Danny hated Spike laughing at him, but Spike continued laughing nevertheless. 'So those kids at school think you're slower than a cheese sandwich, do they?' he said, guffawing.

'No, Spike,' Danny replied tersely. 'They didn't say that.'

'What sort of cheese?' asked Spike, still laughing merrily at his own joke. 'We talking cheddar here, soft cheese, Stilton, or something runny, a cheese that runs, like a Camembert?'

'Very funny, Spike!' Danny replied, making it clear that actually it wasn't funny at all.

'I think I've got a new name for you, Dan,' Spike

continued, laughing to himself. 'No longer Speedboy but "The Camembert Kid".'

'Spike! Don't you get it? Not funny!'

'OK.' Spike stopped laughing immediately, stood up and changed his tone of voice. It was clear now that he was taking this seriously. 'I'm sorry your mates had a laugh at you today. But we've talked about this before, haven't we, Dan?'

'Yes, Spike.'

'No one thinks you've got a chance of beating Usain Bolt, do they?'

'No, Spike.'

'How many people in the entire world actually think you can beat him?'

'Two, Spike.'

'And are they your schoolmates?'

'No, Spike.'

'Who are they then?'

'You and me, Spike.'

'Exactly,' said Spike. 'You and me. No one else knows, and no one else will know that you've got a chance of beating Bolt until May the twentieth. That's the plan, isn't it?'

'Yes, Spike. That's the plan.'

20 May. It was all down to 20 May. In Spike's office was a poster he had made entitled 'Sunday 20 May'. And underneath in big letters was written: '68 days until the Olympics. The Day Danny Powell Shocks the World.' Danny laughed at that because

20 May was the day of the 100-metres final in the UK School Games and Danny didn't think that anyone would take the blindest bit of notice of what went on there. But Spike did. Spike's big plans revolved heavily around 20 May. That would be Danny's first 100 metres of the year and he expected Danny to run faster than Carl and Jesse. That was the plan.

The fact that Carl was fifty years old and Jesse died over ten years before Danny was born was irrelevant. Spike was obsessed with Carl and Jesse. He talked about them so much that they soon became known as Uncle Carl and Uncle Jesse. The reason that Spike was obsessed with Danny being faster than Uncle Carl and Uncle Jesse was because he believed that if you could beat them, then you had a chance of beating Usain too. Because the real identity of Uncle Carl was Carl Lewis and the real identity of Uncle Jesse was Jesse Owens and they were two of the fastest runners of all time. And if you could beat these guys, then you had a chance of beating Bolt.

All this was written in large letters on the poster on Spike's office wall. Towards the bottom of the poster, under 'The Day Danny Powell Shocks the World', there were pictures of Carl Lewis and Jesse Owens and a series of numbers next to their names. These numbers were the fastest times they had ever run over 100 metres, but they were not just their all-time personal fastest times, but their progression, their fastest time when they were twenty-one years old, their fastest time when they were twenty and their fastest time when they were eighteen.

Spike thought it was important that Danny knew how fast Uncle Carl and Uncle Jesse were when they were eighteen because then Danny could compare himself, almost as if he was running against them. He wanted Danny to come away from the UK School Games believing that he was faster than the two greatest legends of the sport.

So these are the facts that stared out at Danny from the poster on Spike's wall:

- Jesse Owens, aged nineteen, personal best: 10.40 seconds.
- Carl Lewis, aged eighteen, personal best: 10.29 seconds.
- Danny Powell, aged seventeen, personal best: 10.41 seconds.

Personal bests, it was all about personal bests. Or PBs as everyone called them. Every sprinter knows his PB. Every sprinter is trying to better his PB. Every sprinter wants his PB to be better than everyone else's. Your PB tells you and everyone else how good you are. At least that is the way Spike told it.

'The thing is,' said Spike, 'that the ignorant cheese-sandwich brigade at your school don't know what we know.' He was now pointing to the poster, jabbing the numbers on it with his index finger. 'That cheese-sandwich brigade don't understand that when you were seventeen, your PB was almost as fast as the great Carl Lewis when he was eighteen, and not far off the great Jesse Owens when he was nineteen.

'May the twentieth will be your first run of the season, your first 100 metres as an eighteen-year-old and I know how fast you can go and how much more speed you've got in your legs since last year. If you run a new PB on May the twentieth the way I know you can, then you'll have Uncle Carl and Uncle Jesse on toast. You'll sail past them. And that, Speedboy, will shove the cheese sandwiches right back down the throats of your mates at school.'

Danny was quiet. He loved hearing Spike talking like this. Spike gave him the confidence he needed. Spike made him want to prove everyone wrong, to show them just how good he was and how wrong they were, to wipe the clever little smiles off their faces, to show everyone at Newham Secondary that his dream wasn't so stupid after all. When Spike talked like this, it made Danny feel angry, excited, determined and, best of all, confident: confident that he could have his two favourite uncles on toast.

'Come on then, Spike,' Danny said, rising to his feet. 'Let's go train.'

'Good lad,' Spike said, punching him affection-
ately on the shoulder. 'I hope you've brought your
speed with you today. Because I am about to kill
you.'

★ 5 ★

TWO UNCLES AND A BROTHER

Spike may have lost his chance to be a sprinter, but he still loved the sport. In fact, Danny wondered if maybe the very reason that Spike loved it so much was because he never actually got his own chance. Either way, the end result was that Spike insisted that Danny showed respect for sprinting.

Spike loved the sport so much that he couldn't stand it when he saw young athletes who did not. Spike hated the new breed of cocky young guns that had risen to the top level and behaved as though they were God's gift. 'The swaggerers,' Spike would call them because of the way they would strut around as if they ruled the world.

So Spike loved Danny – because he saw that Danny was different; he was modest, humble and respectful of the sport. Danny was the opposite of a swaggerer. 'Speed is special,' Spike would say. 'If you've been blessed with it, you have to honour it.'

And that is why Danny came to know Uncle Carl and Uncle Jesse as if they really were his relations.

This guy was probably the coolest athlete of all time. At least in Danny's opinion he was.

Some days, when training had gone well, Spike would take Danny back into his office and show him a YouTube film of Jesse Owens. There were only a few short clips and Danny noticed that Spike's eyes would sometimes moisten as he watched them. Spike loved and admired Uncle Jesse so much it almost made him cry.

The film was only black and white and there were only clips from the 1936 Olympics. Those were the Olympics when Owens shocked the world. They were held in Berlin, the capital of Germany, three years before the Second World War, at a time when the power of Adolf Hitler, the German dictator, was growing fast. Those Olympic Games were strange because of Hitler, who wanted to use the Olympics to try to prove to the rest of the world how powerful he was and how his German nation was the best. Hitler saw sport and the Olympics as a mini-version of war; he wanted Germany to rule the world.

So Hitler was desperate for the German athletes to win absolutely everything. However, he had not accounted for Uncle Jesse who would turn out to be the star of the show. The 'king of kings', as Spike would call him.

Jesse Owens was a black American kid whose family were poor and whose grandfather had been a slave. When he was only seven, Jesse himself had to work as a labourer picking cotton in the fields. But, at school, it soon became clear that Jesse was something very special. And, when Jesse went to the Berlin Olympics, it also became clear that, despite whatever Hitler had hoped for, Jesse would be the star of the Games.

His first gold medal was for the 100 metres. This was the one that Spike kept showing Danny on YouTube. When you watch the clip, you can see a look of nervousness on Jesse's face at the start as he waited for the gun to fire. You can even see him swallowing; in fact, he seems to swallow so hard that he suddenly looks more nervous than before. But then the gun goes off and he is ahead almost immediately, and no one comes close to catching him.

After that, Jesse won the long jump, then the 200 metres. 'And don't forget,' Spike would remind Danny, 'that he not only won the 200 metres, he broke the Olympic record at the same time.' And Jesse then finished by being part of the American team to win the sprint relay.

'Four gold medals for Uncle Jesse,' Spike told him. 'And Hitler hated every single one of them. You know, Hitler hated Uncle Jesse's gold medals so much that he refused to congratulate him afterwards. Everyone else in Berlin seemed to love Uncle Jesse.

Whenever he was out on the streets, he was surrounded by fans who wanted his autograph. Some of them even found out where his room was and they posted their autograph books through the letter box when he was asleep.

'He was a true hero, Speedboy. But think about how hard it was: he was working in the fields when he was seven! How do you go from that to being Olympic champion? And he had Hitler against him too. He had people forever making his life hard. But he wouldn't let that stop him or get him down. What a triumph, and if you can be as good as Uncle Jesse, as noble and true to yourself and as fast too, then you could be a hero one day too.'

2. UNCLE CARL

The thing about sprinting – at least, this was another of the many things about sprinting that Spike liked to tell Danny – is that you are always chasing or being chased. If you catch the guy in front of you, then you can guarantee that there will be someone on your tail trying to catch you.

'You can never relax,' Spike told him. 'You can never rest on your laurels. The minute you sit back and think that you rule the world, that's the minute that someone else will come and catch you.'

Uncle Carl was amazing because he kept on going

and going. And, when he did get caught, he simply redoubled his efforts and got to the front again.

Uncle Carl was another black American. He grew up knowing all about Jesse Owens and all he wanted to do was copy him. And the thing about Uncle Carl was that when he decided he wanted to do something he pretty much always managed it.

So at the Olympics in 1984, when Carl was twenty-three, he competed in four events. They were the same four events in which Uncle Jesse had competed forty-eight years earlier. And, like Uncle Jesse, Uncle Carl won every single one of them.

But Uncle Carl was not done there. He won two more gold medals at the next Olympics in 1988, two more after that in the 1992 Olympics, and, in 1996, when he was thirty-five and everyone was telling him that he was too old, he proved them all wrong by winning one more, in the long jump. In fact, Uncle Carl won the long jump for four Olympic Games running.

Uncle Carl was also pretty cool, but in a strange kind of way. He was cool because he didn't care what people thought about him. He once appeared in an advert for car tyres wearing a pair of ladies' red, high-heeled shoes. 'Everyone thought he was crazy,' Spike said. 'Everyone laughed at him. But that's what I liked about him, Dan: he simply didn't care.'

And this was the lesson for Danny: be like Carl, be strong in your mind. People thought Carl was strange because of the ladies' red shoes, but he didn't let that bother him. And people thought he was too old to win an Olympic medal in 1996, but he didn't care about that either. He simply believed in himself.

As Danny left the Lee Valley Stadium later that afternoon, Spike again talked to him about Uncle Carl. 'Imagine what it would be like if Uncle Carl was at your school, Dan,' Spike told him. 'Uncle Carl was a real show-off. Can you imagine what those idiots in your class would think of him?'

'Sure can, Spike,' Danny replied.

'And do you think he would care?' Spike asked.

'Nope.'

'Do you think he would believe them if they told him that he was slower than a cheese sandwich?'

'Nope.'

'Exactly,' Spike said, putting a hand on Danny's shoulder. 'Look, Speedboy, if Carl was you, he'd be looking at those school kids and laughing to himself. He'd be thinking: "I will prove them wrong. I will wipe the smug little smiles off their cheesy faces. Because I know how good I am and they haven't got the faintest clue." Wouldn't he, Dan?'

'Yes, Spike.'

'Good. Now go home. Eat. Do your homework and go to bed. And before you go to sleep, think about Uncle Carl. Because when you start to think like him, that's when you might start running like him too.'

3. BROTHER RICKY

Carl and Jesse were never Danny's real uncles and they never would be. But, though Ricky was Danny's real brother, there were times when Danny wondered if they were really related at all. Ricky was three years older, but he now seemed a brother from another lifetime.

Back in the old days, they used to be so close. Ricky, Danny and Anthuan were a tight-knit group, a trio of superstar athletes, all being killed together on a daily basis by Spike. They would train together, sweat together, watch athletics on the TV together, talk about athletics together and then they would go to sleep thinking about athletics too.

But people always go their separate ways. Anthuan gradually grew bored of the regime; he didn't want to train all the time, every afternoon. He wanted to be free to hang out with their other mates. He slowly drifted away and then, one day, Spike asked him very gently if he really wanted to be an athlete or if he wanted to quit. And he chose to quit. It wasn't an angry exchange, but Spike had seen that Anthuan had lost his love for the track, and, if you are trying to run as fast as Danny and Ricky and Anthuan, you either love it or you don't bother. It's all or nothing. And, when pushed, Anthuan was happy to choose nothing.

But Ricky was different. Ricky was astonishingly fast, immensely talented, probably the most talented of all three of them. Danny grew up always wondering if he would ever be as fast as him. He felt absolutely certain that his brother would one day run in the Olympics. He looked up to him; he loved him and he loved it that Ricky looked after him and encouraged him so much. But then Ricky said he was quitting too.

Danny hated that day. Ricky explained over and over: 'I'm going to university in Liverpool. I need to pursue my life, my career, and I can't do that here with Spike and, if I can't have Spike, I can't be a runner any more.'

And so Ricky left for Liverpool, but it was strange. It didn't seem that he was just a couple of hundred miles away; it seemed instead as if he had gone to the other side of the world. Ricky rarely called home and he hardly ever texted. Their parents said they were proud of him: the first member of the family ever to go to university, and he was probably working too hard to call. But that wasn't quite good enough for Danny.

And, as Danny grew older and faster, the silences grew and the bond between Ricky and him just faded further. After every race, Danny would always text Ricky to tell him the result and his time. He thought that, if nothing else, they would always be bonded by their love for athletics. But rarely did he get a reply.

There were times when Danny just felt like giving up on his big brother. But he loved him too much and he wanted Ricky to love him back. So he resolved not to give up, never to stop. So he made it his own private rule: *after every race you ever run, always, always text Ricky*.

That was why he was hoping for a reply from Ricky today. *Always text Ricky*. So he had texted Ricky yesterday to tell him about his race with the thief. He thought Ricky might like that. But no, no reply.

Ricky may have gone quiet, but one day, maybe, he'd turn the volume up again.

★ 6 ★

FRIDAY NIGHT FEVER

Friday nights are meant for fun. That is what Ant told Danny. Ant was telling him this a lot these days. Maybe he was right.

These were Danny's thoughts as he sat at his desk in his bedroom with a pad full of history revision notes on his right and a book about Hitler's rise to power to his left. This was one of the subjects he enjoyed most because it helped him understand Uncle Jesse a little better, but still: history revision or the movies? He knew where he would rather be.

He looked at his phone and the last text from Ant, forty-five minutes ago:

> We're going to be meeting at the usual place if you change your mind.

'Love to,' Danny replied. 'Same old answer.'

The same old answer was this: I have two priorities, the two As: A levels and athletics. Unfortunately, nothing else gets a look-in.

After he left school, Danny's parents expected him

41

to go to university like Ricky. His father always wanted him to be like Ricky. Danny quite wanted to be like Ricky too, but give up running? Never.

Danny looked at the history book. When exams came round, he hoped he would get the chance to write about 1936 and Hitler's Olympics. Surprise, surprise, this was his specialist subject. He loved the story of Jesse Owens in the long jump: how Hitler looked down upon Owens's victory with disgust, but how the German who won the silver medal, Luz Long, came up to Owens and warmly congratulated him. That was a brave thing that Long did. Just briefly, Owens and Long then became friends – and, a few years later, Long would die in the Second World War. And, in the years that followed, Owens made an effort to stay in contact with Long's family. Amazing story.

Danny wondered about the Olympics. *If I go, will I have a story? Will I go? And what will Usain Bolt be like?*

Danny looked again at his revision notes. *Come on, get on with your work!*

But it's hard to work when you are running the biggest race of your life the next day. Spike was going to pick him up because his parents couldn't make it. Usually, they travelled all round England to watch him in action, but not on this occasion – because they had already gone up to Liverpool to see Ricky. It was Ricky's birthday.

Ricky's birthday versus the biggest race of your life – what's more important? *Unfair question*, thought Danny. *After all, it's not even as though Mum and Dad really know exactly what tomorrow is all about.*

Danny looked again at his revision notes. *Come on, get on with your work!*

★ 7 ★

20 MAY

No one else knew that 20 May was so important. No one had a clue. They certainly did not know that Danny Powell's coach had a poster of it on his wall.

The day before, the Saturday, Spike and Danny had driven up to Sheffield in Spike's rather uncool, blue Ford Focus. Danny was unusually quiet, though that wasn't because of the nerves but because of the texts he was getting from Anthuan.

> You missed a great night last night.

And:

> Dead cool movie.

And then a while later:

> Good luck in Sheffield. I know how important it is to you.

But Danny did start to feel nervous too. He became aware of himself whenever he swallowed – like Uncle Jesse. And then he told himself that he didn't care – like Uncle Carl. And afterwards he felt a little better.

The UK School Games was the biggest school sports event in the whole of the year. Danny thought it must be like a mini-Olympics. There were thousands of competitors and pretty much every single competitor seemed to have a coach or a parent with them, or two parents, or even the whole lot. And every single boy and girl there felt that this was the biggest day of their lives.

The Don Valley Stadium in Sheffield was an awesome venue for the athletics. It could seat 25,000 spectators. Danny found himself blinking in amazement as he and Spike walked in. And then he swallowed and felt that nervousness run through him again. But swallowing is all right – at least that is what he told himself. That is what Uncle Jesse did, and he was the king of kings.

The day before a race, the night before, even a few hours before it, Danny would feel nervous. And that was when he and Spike would play chess, whenever possible, about three hours before a race. They would go to the venue, sit down somewhere quiet and Spike would bring out the chessboard. This was Spike's way of helping Danny take his mind off the race, to kill the nerves a bit. And Danny liked this; he loved going head to head with Spike on the chessboard and watching Spike getting competitive, so desperate and determined to win. He had never, ever beaten Spike at chess. Not once. But defeat on the chessboard seemed to set him up perfectly for victory on the track.

Danny liked the routine and the way it helped him. It went like this: nerves, chess, less nerves, warm-up, no nerves.

As the race got close, Danny seemed to change. He liked this change; it was as if he was becoming a different person, as if he was changing from Danny Powell into Speedboy. He would feel less and less. nervous and more and more confident. He felt belief sweeping through him. He felt sure he could win.

There were now about two minutes until the start of the race. When you stand at the startline of a race like this, the whole world seems to stand still. At least that is what Danny always felt. You know that the crowd is large and you know they are making a lot of noise, but you don't hear anything. All you hear is your heart beating.

Danny sat down on the ground to try and compose himself. There are eight people in a 100-metres final and Danny thought, when he looked hard at all the other seven, that he could detect an element of nerv-ousness in all their faces, in the way they were behaving. *Good*, he thought, *because a nervous athlete is more likely to make mistakes.*

Danny knew five of the other seven already; he had raced them enough times before and he was pretty confident he could beat them. And his PB was better than all the other seven lined up here. He hadn't lost a race against other boys his own age for four years, so why start now?

He looked over to Jimmy Lewis, the Welsh kid. Jimmy was tying and untying his shoelaces. He tied them again, then untied them and then tied them again. Jimmy always did this; he said it was a nervous habit that helped him concentrate. But it made Danny laugh; Danny liked Jimmy, but he was also wary of him because he knew that Jimmy was good, probably his biggest threat. He knew that Jimmy, on a good day, could push him. But he also knew that he had one thing that Jimmy wanted: a brilliant start.

Jimmy was taller than Danny and had longer legs and a longer stride. Theoretically, Jimmy should have been brilliant. But if you are going to be a world-class sprinter, then your reactions have to be razor-sharp; the very millisecond that the gun goes to start the race, you have to be powering off, your legs pumping hard to try and build your speed.

But while Jimmy's start was good, Danny's was brilliant. It is vital to start explosively quickly and Danny always exploded like a rocket.

He knew the race routine so well he could do it with his eyes closed. At the start of a race, when they announce 'On your marks', you step forward to the line and put your feet into your blocks – the steel blocks screwed into the ground. Then you wait, rest your feet in the blocks, try to be calm, tense but calm, and get that feeling that you are a coiled spring. And then, when the gun goes for the start of the race, you unleash the spring; you push off from the blocks with all the power you can summon.

The power of Danny's spring was immense and he knew it. Today he would have to be as powerful as ever.

But here is why 20 May was so important. At least this was how Spike had explained it, over and over again. It wasn't about winning the race – though that would of course be nice. It was all about the time in which Danny could win it. It was about how fast he could be. Because Danny's PB over 100 metres was 10.41 seconds and today he needed to go under 10.20 seconds. Because if he got under 10.20 seconds, then he would qualify to run at the British Olympic trials. And if he finished first or second in the British Olympic trials, then he would get a place in the Great Britain team for the Olympics.

Simple. Or maybe not. But that was the plan.

As those final seconds before the race ticked away, Spike whispered in Danny's ear, 'Good luck, Speed-boy. Your Olympic dream starts here.' And Danny knew exactly what he meant.

My Olympic dream! That was the thought racing through Danny's head. *Bring it on!*

'On your marks.'

There was the loud announcement, interrupting Danny's thought pattern and bringing all the runners to the startline. Danny went to his lane, crouched down in the starting position, put his feet back into the blocks and looked ahead down the track.

'Set.'

This was the last call before the gun. Danny raised himself slightly, ready to burst out of his blocks.

Bang!

The gun went and all eight runners burst out of their starting positions.

Bang!

The gun went again.

Again? Not again! Please not again.

But it had. That was the second gun blast that every sprinter feared.

So Danny stopped running and the other seven runners around him stopped too. They all knew what happened next and they all feared it.

Someone was going to be disqualified.

That is the horrible, harsh reality of sprinting at this level. You have to have those razor-sharp reactions; you have got to move like lightning the very split-second that the gun has been fired. But a fast start is so hugely important that sometimes people just get it wrong. Almost every first-class sprinter that has ever lived has got it wrong once or twice in their career. It is called a 'false start' – which means that you have started running before the gun has gone off.

It's a horrible mistake, but so easy to make – you're there in your blocks, poised, the adrenalin is pumping;

you're nervous, excited, like a wound-up coil ready to be sprung. And so sometimes the springs go early – before the gun. You go and then the gun goes after you. And the new rules in Danny's sport are so unforgiving, that one false start means the end. Disqualification. You are not allowed to run the race. It is an excruciatingly horrible way to lose.

That is why the sport is so hard. Because you can train all year, you can make all those sacrifices – and then you can waste it all on one tiny mistake.

And so when Danny and the other seven in the 100-metres final in the Don Valley Stadium heard that second bang, they all thought: *Oh, please, please, let it not be me.* Danny was pretty sure that it wasn't him. But he also knew the facts of the matter: *If I have false-started, then that's my Olympic dream over here and now.*

He walked slowly back to the startline and, just before he got there, there was a stadium announcement: 'False start. The runner in Lane Two. Lenny Passmore is disqualified.'

Danny turned to watch Lenny. He had seen him a couple of times before. He seemed a decent guy. But he had never seen him like this: angry, disbelieving and crying. Big tears rolled down his face. He refused to leave the race. He shouted at one of the officials. He protested his innocence. But then, eventually, he was led away; his hopes and dreams left in tatters on the track.

And then there were seven. Back on the startline again. Trying to concentrate again. Trying to forget about Lenny Passmore and the fate of the false-starter. Trying to run the race of their lives.

'On your marks!'

'Set.'

Bang!

This time the gun went only once.

Danny felt confident and strong. A good, powerful start. But what he hadn't expected was that Jimmy's start would be even better.

Never look at your rivals. Never look to one side or the other. Always look ahead. That was one of the key rules that every young sprinter learns before they even become teenagers. But Danny didn't need to look at his rivals to know, thirty metres into the race, that Jimmy was ahead. Jimmy had got the best start of his life. *Jimmy's in front of me. What's Jimmy doing there?* The thought raced through Danny's mind.

But the 100 metres is so quick and so fast that you barely have time to think. You just have to concentrate. *Pump the knees high. Concentrate. Feel the speed.*

At the sixty-metre mark, Danny was neck and neck with Jimmy. He felt he was flying, as though his feet were barely touching the ground. *Come on, Dan, pump the knees, high and hard.* At eighty metres, he wasn't sure if he was ahead. He felt Jimmy right by him.

Danny powered on through the line. *I've got it*, he thought. *I've definitely got it.* By centimetres, he was the champion. Again.

But that hardly mattered. What mattered was the time on the big scoreboard clock. And the clock showed that he had just run the 100 metres in a time of 10.17 seconds. He had smashed his own PB. He had beaten both Uncle Carl and Uncle Jesse too. By quite some way. But, most importantly, he had run fast enough to qualify for the Olympic trials.

Danny collapsed on to the ground and looked up at the sky. *The Olympic dream was still alive!* And there was a massive smile on his face. He felt the warm rays of the sun upon him. Momentarily, he felt very, very happy. *The Olympics! Usain Bolt!* The thoughts started charging through his mind – until he was interrupted by a loud Welsh voice.

'Oy! You! Superstar! Get up, man!' It was Jimmy Lewis. 'Get up, man! You must be the fastest oaf on the planet!'

Jimmy held out his hand to Danny who grabbed it and Jimmy hauled Danny back up to his feet. 'Well done, Dan! Great run,' Jimmy said.

'I thought you had me there, Jim,' Danny replied.

'Yeah, best start of my life and I still couldn't beat you.'

Danny looked up at the scoreboard. Their times had vanished from the screen. 'What time did you do, Jimmy?' he asked.

'I did a personal best, a great big juicy PB,' he replied. 'Can you believe it? 10.19 seconds!'

Danny swivelled round and put his hands on Jimmy's shoulders so he could look him straight in the face. 'You know what that means?' Danny asked.

'Yeah,' Jimmy replied nonchalantly. 'It means you're still faster than me.'

'No, Jimmy, you nutter!' Danny said. 'Listen. 10.19 seconds. You've qualified for the Olympic trials. You and me, Jimmy, Olympic trials! We could be going to the Olympics!'

'And you call me a nutter!' Jimmy replied. 'Try looking in the mirror and saying that and you will realize how stupid it sounds.'

'I do say it,' Danny replied. 'Almost every day. And it doesn't sound stupid at all.'

★ 8 ★

SERIOUS SPIKE

By the time Spike had dropped Danny home, it was late. They had not hung around the Don Valley Stadium long because they knew they had a big drive ahead of them. They simply waited for Danny to collect his medal, grab a quick shower and then off they went, laughing and cheering down the motorway for all of about twelve minutes.

Spike wasn't into celebrations. He didn't like the applause or all the patting on the back. But Danny didn't care. He got into Spike's Ford Focus and didn't stop talking. He talked about the start of the race, the middle of the race and the end of the race. He talked about the forthcoming Olympic trials and then he talked about the Olympics and then he talked about Usain Bolt. He was so excited he could hardly be bothered to notice that he was doing all the talking and it was Spike who kept his eyes glued to the road, barely registering the triumph that his Speedboy had just pulled off.

'Come on, Spike!' Danny said eventually – after

about twelve minutes of non-stop gassing. 'Enjoy the moment.'

'No,' Spike replied. 'You enjoy the moment because you're entitled to. But me? I can only think ahead. I'm pleased with the way you ran today, Dan. But I won't lie to you. I'm pleased, but only *quite* pleased. I'm a long way from being *very* pleased. You made a couple of mistakes out there today, Dan. Your start wasn't good. Jimmy Lewis nearly had you. In fact, your start was very average indeed. But you ran a good time; you got the time you needed. So that's why I'm pleased.'

'So can't we enjoy that for more than twelve minutes, Spike? What's the problem?' Danny asked, a bit confused.

'The problem is this, Dan. You've just done the easy bit. You've qualified for the Olympic trials. That's the easy bit. But you cannot afford to celebrate as if the job's been done. It hasn't. It just gets harder from here. The Olympic trials will be harder than today, much harder. And then the Olympics? Well, you haven't the faintest clue what that will be like. You ran well today, Dan, but you've got to get so, so, so, so much better.'

And that was Spike through and through. Danny wasn't surprised, just a bit miffed. *What more can I do?* he thought to himself. *Am I supposed to train any more? Because I can't. I do not have enough hours in my day. Must I make more sacrifices? I have no more to make.*

So they drove on in silence. Danny texted Ricky with his news: the victory, his new PB and the qualification for the Olympic trials. He wondered to himself, *What is the point?* but he sent the text nevertheless.

He received another text from his mum:

Come on, Dan! Tell us what happened. Your father and I are desperate to know.

'Home soon,' Danny replied. 'Will tell all then.' Danny laughed to himself; he loved his parents, but he also loved to tease them. And then he plugged himself into his iPod, sat back and tried to replay the race in his mind. He liked doing that.

But any remnants of joy that survived the three hours in Spike's Ford Focus would soon be stamped out altogether. At 10.45 p.m., Spike dropped Danny off, shook his hand meaningfully and said to him in a serious voice, 'Well done, Dan. Honestly, well done. The dream is still alive.'

But then Danny put his key into the door of his house and soon realized that he may as well not have bothered with the dream at all.

★ 9 ★

A LEVELS OR OLYMPICS?

Danny's parents had got back from Liverpool earlier and waited up for him. They were sitting in the front room having a cup of tea. They were all fidgety and excited because they didn't know the result of the race and the minute Danny walked in, they both got to their feet. Danny's mum rushed over to him and took his bag, his dad stood stock-still and they both said in unison: 'How did you go? How did you go?'

'Not bad,' Danny replied, nodding his head, the big smile back on his face, playing it slightly cool. 'Not bad!'

'Oh, come on,' said his mum frustratedly. 'Spill the beans. Your father and I have been dying to know. Why didn't you text me? You cruel boy!'

So Danny sat down on the sofa in the front room and talked them through his race from beginning to end. He told them about the nightmare false start, about Jimmy, the start, about how he chased Jimmy and caught him, and about his time. His personal best, his new PB, 10.17 seconds. And throughout neither his mum nor his dad said a single word.

And finally he knew it was time to tell them what this all meant. He had not dared tell them before because he never wanted to let them down. He never wanted to promise anything he couldn't deliver. So he had kept it to himself that he thought he could run in the Olympics. But now was his chance. Danny felt excited and proud. He paused and then started speaking.

'The dream goes on.'

'What do you mean, Dan?' his father replied.

'You know what's going to happen now?' he said, sitting forward in the sofa. 'You know that magnificent Olympic Park just a few hundred metres away from us? You know the big stadium? The one where they'll hold all the athletics in the Olympics? The one that Anthuan and I, when we're messing around, call "Bolt's Second Home"?'

'Yes,' his parents replied in unison.

'Well, I'm going to run there in three weeks' time.'

'How come?' they asked, still in unison and slightly overexcited.

And so Danny explained. He explained first about the Olympic trials and about the qualifying time that was needed to run in them. With 10.17 seconds, he would be able to run in the trials. In three weeks' time, right here in the Olympic Stadium. And if he came first or second in the trials, then he would qualify for the Olympics.

Danny's mum seemed thrilled. She stood up and sat down again. Then she stood up again. She didn't know what to do with herself. So she sat down next to Danny. 'You clever boy!' she said, kissing him on the forehead. 'I am so proud of you. So, so proud.'

But Danny's dad did not respond in the same way. Not at all. In fact, he just stayed seated and said nothing. When Danny's mum realized that he wasn't sharing her joy, she went quiet and both she and Danny looked at him as if waiting for an answer.

'What is it, Dad?' Danny asked. 'I'm going to run in the Olympic Stadium. That's kind of cool, isn't it?'

'I just need a bit more information,' said his dad.

'OK, what do you need to know?'

'Well,' his dad said, slowly and seriously. 'These Olympic trials are a big deal, right?'

'Right.'

'Are they the biggest deal of your whole life? Will this be the biggest and most important race you have ever run?'

'Oh yes, without a doubt.'

'And,' his dad paused and carried on, 'because you are proud and because you've worked hard for your success as a sprinter, I take it that you'll be training hard for these trials, yes?'

59

'Absolutely. Spike is going to be killing me in training pretty much every day.'

'Right.' His dad then stopped and shook his head as if something was wrong.

'What is it, Dad?' Danny asked. He was now completely confused.

His dad said nothing and the silence was so complete that you could hear the clock ticking on the mantelpiece. Then, eventually, he sat forward and continued: 'OK. A couple more questions. One: while you've been up in Sheffield winning running races this weekend, what have your mates been up to?'

'I don't know,' Danny replied. 'Revising, I guess.'

'Revising for what?' his dad asked.

'For A levels.'

'And, Danny, when are your A levels?'

Danny's heart began to sink. He could see where his father was taking this conversation and he didn't like it. 'They start in two weeks' time and they finish the week after the trials,' he replied.

'And you want to do the trials?' His dad stood up and looked out at the street. He was now talking to Danny with his back turned. 'I'm sorry, Danny, but I just don't get this. You have the biggest, most important exams in your life coming up and you want to go and run? You're facing a set of exams that may influence the future course of the whole of your life. If you do well – and you should do well, you deserve to do well – you'll go to university. And you want to spend your every spare minute up at Lee Valley being killed by Spike?'

Danny looked at his mother for help, but it was clear he wasn't going to get it. She gave him a weak and apologetic smile.

'Dad, I can do both,' Danny replied.

His dad sighed deeply, paused and then turned back to Danny. 'Dan, you know that we love you and you know that we support you and we have so much admiration for the work and love that you put into your running. You know that, don't you, Dan?'

'Yes, Dad.'

'But you know, and I know, that you cannot do both. If you do both, you'll do neither to your best. Do you want to run and not win? Do you want to sit your exams and not do your very, very best? I don't think you do, Dan. If you study hard for your exams, then you won't have time to train and you never win races like that. And, if you train hard, then you won't have time to study and you'll screw up the exams.'

There was another prolonged silence. Danny didn't know what to say. Eventually, his father started speaking again. 'I'm sorry, Dan, I'm really sorry. But your exams have got to come first.'

'And the Olympics?'

'I know you want to run in the Olympics. That's always been your dream. But not these Olympics!

The Olympic Games will come round again in four years' time.'

'But they won't be here. They won't be right on our doorstep.'

'I know, Dan. I know.'

'But Dad! I could do both. I promise I could do both. I swear I can.' There was now a slightly desperate tone to Danny's voice. 'I'll do nothing else for three weeks: train and study, train and study. Nothing else, Dad. Nothing else. That's all I do anyway.'

An awkward silence now filled the room.

Then his father spoke again. 'Look at your brother Ricky, Dan. Look at him, a successful young man studying at university. Do you think he would be where he is if he'd decided to go running during his A levels?'

'Ricky?' Dan couldn't believe that his father was using Ricky to make his point.

'Yes, Dan, you don't get where Ricky has got by being a part-time student.'

'But I don't want to be like Ricky. He gave up running. I can't give it up. I'm a runner. I can't change that.'

His father paused again. 'Danny, do you want to go to university?'

Dan sighed. He was in a corner and he could see there was no way out of it. 'Yes,' he said wearily.

'Well then . . .' his father said quietly. He knew his point had been made.

An awkward silence ensued. They could hear the mantelpiece clock ticking again and the noise of a car engine out on the street. And Danny didn't know what to say; he didn't know what to do. He had never considered this. Never had he ventured to think that his dad would take against him. He felt stupid. He felt as though his dad was ripping something important away from him and he felt really, really angry. This was his life, his dream. He knew his dad was right; he knew that his A levels were important. But he was absolutely, 100 per cent convinced that he could do both.

'You've got to give me a break on this, Dad,' he said quietly, pleadingly.

'I cannot tell you how much I would like to,' his dad said. 'But I can't.'

'Mum?' Danny asked, hopeful that she might take his side.

But his mother slowly shook her head. She had a sad look on her face and eventually spoke: 'I'm sorry, Dan. But you know your father's right.'

Danny looked at his father, as if he had one last hope, and then back to his mother, as if she might provide it instead. But he got the same negative reaction from both. At that point, Danny could keep calm no longer. He was furious and he leaped to his feet.

'Right!' he shouted at his parents. He even surprised himself with how loud and angry he sounded. 'Have it your way. It's over. The dream is finished. My life, my dream. Finished!'

'Come on, Dan!' said his mum, trying to reassure him. 'It's just one Olympics. There'll be more. You'll have another chance.'

'No!' he replied, louder even than before. 'You don't get it, do you? This is my chance. Now. Right now. I might never be this good again. I might be injured in four years' time. I might not be so fast. I might be fat and overweight. I don't know what I might be. All I know is that now I am ready. Now is my time. And you two are denying me the dream of my life. Thank you very much indeed!'

And, with that, he walked straight over to the front door, stepped outside and slammed it loudly behind him.

★ 10 ★

DREAM OR REALITY?

It was cold outside, but Danny didn't feel it. All he felt was anger and frustration. And confusion. He started walking down the street, but he didn't know where he was going. Then he started running and he still didn't know where he was going.

And all the time, round and round and round in his head, there kept spinning the same nagging questions. *What's more important: A levels or Olympics? Studies or sport? Going to university? Or going to the biggest and best athletics meetings in the world and earning a living from it?* And there then followed more questions: *If someone offered me a deal where I could beat Usain Bolt and be Olympic champion, but, at the same time, failed all my A levels – would I take that? Was that worth it?* And then came another question: *Am I just kidding myself? If Usain Bolt can finish the 100 metres and then eat a cheese sandwich ahead of me, then maybe this whole debate is a colossal waste of time and energy.*

But one thing was certain: to his father, there was no confusion. A levels came before Olympics. End of story. Simple. And that then led to the other thought bouncing round Danny's mind: *Maybe Dad is right . . .*

Danny's dad – Elroy, or Roy to most people – was the kind of guy that everyone respected. He had a few good friends, but more noticeable was the respect that he commanded. Whatever he talked about, he always spoke wisely. Sometimes he wouldn't say much, but, when he did speak, he had this presence and people would listen. He seemed to have authority. He was straightforward, logical, level-headed – in other words, he was everything that an eighteen-year-old boy with crazy Olympic dreams didn't need right now. He was so infuriatingly sensible, Danny felt he wanted to throttle him.

But Roy's authority was well earned. He had not had an easy life. He was born in Jamaica, the very same Caribbean island that Bolt himself came from. But Roy had no memories of Jamaica because, when he was three years old, his parents came to London in search of work and a new life. Except Roy's father found that he didn't like the work or the life and so, within a year, he went back home to Jamaica. And that was the end of his father. His father had said he would come back soon, but he never did. Not so much as a flying visit. His mother, Juanita, kept photographs of him for Roy to look at, to remind him where he came from. But neither Juanita nor Roy ever heard from him again.

So Roy was brought up by Juanita, and Juanita alone. She worked hard to give him the food and clothing and the love he required and it was through her that he learned the lessons that would forever guide him: that the skills required to build a good home and a happy life were hard work and honesty.

And, as Danny wandered through the streets that night, he began cursing Juanita. *Was it her fault that he had a father who was so completely and utterly and unswervingly sensible? Was it her fault that his father wanted to stop him going to the Olympics?* He smiled to himself at the thought of Juanita – his splendid, loving grandmother. She had died when he was ten, but he treasured her memory dearly. She would have loved to have seen him running in the Olympics, here on their doorstep. So he couldn't and wouldn't blame her. And, come to think of it, it was hard to blame his dad too.

It was now nearly midnight and, without really thinking about where he was going or what he was doing, Danny found himself on Bridge Road, the best spot in Stratford, where he and Anthuan would come to stand and gaze at the enormous Olympic Park. Danny stopped now and stared. There were a few lights on in the park and he found himself imagining what it would be like on 27 July when the Olympic Games finally started. *What would it be like to be there? Sixty-eight days to go. What would it be like to be in the main Olympic stadium running the final of the 100 metres? And would his father come to watch?*

His father had always loved watching him run. When they were small, his father used to take the two boys to West Ham Park and race them. They would set up mini-racetracks, from the cycle path to the tree, to the tree and back again. Ricky v. Dad, Danny v. Dad, Ricky v. Danny – that was the one that Danny really liked, the one he tried so hard in. Anything, anything to beat his brother, but he could never come close.

And sometimes his father would take off his watch and time the boys separately and then coo in admiration at how fast they had gone. 'One more time, Dad! One more time! Let us try and break the record,' would be his and Ricky's excitable cries to their father and he would laugh at their never-ending supply of energy. Danny loved those memories.

But they were too precious. His father would only take them running when work allowed him to. His father always put work first. He had worked all his life in the Royal Mail and he was proud of the way he had done it. He had started as a postman. And then, after a few years, he was offered a job in the sorting office. He was good in the sorting office – his boss noticed how hard he worked and how people around him liked to work with him – and so Roy got promoted again and put in charge of a team of workers. And, eventually, he became the boss of the whole branch. And now he had forty-five people working under him. They all liked and respected him. And Roy never wanted to work anywhere else; he liked being loyal to his job; he liked knowing that every month he was going to be able to provide his family with more than they needed. He liked safety, security and stability.

In other words, everything that Roy liked was the opposite to everything that Danny wanted to do with his life right now. Roy liked safe and sensible, but Danny wanted to take a chance, the chance of a lifetime. He knew that running in the Olympics wasn't sensible. He knew that his father's attitude was probably the correct one. But he didn't want to let the dream go. He couldn't. This was the Olympics. His Olympics. On his doorstep.

As Danny stood on Bridge Road, looking over at the Olympic Park, he made up his mind. There and then he decided. He couldn't and wouldn't let his father stop him running. He had to run. He had a dream and nothing was going to stop him pursuing it.

★ 11 ★

THE PLAN

Danny stood out in the cold dark of the night, throwing small pebbles up at Anthuan's bedroom window. It was now half past midnight and he didn't want to wake Ant's parents. He threw two, three, four stones and then a dim light came on in the room and a hand was shuffling around at the curtains, eventually drawing them back. Ant's face peered out and he saw Danny standing in the street. Twenty seconds later, the front door opened and Ant ushered Danny in.

'What on earth are you doing here, Dan?' he asked.

'It's a long, long story,' Danny replied. 'Can I come in?'

'Of course you can.'

'Can I stay the night?'

Ant looked concerned. 'Sure, no prob.'

'I need your help.'

'Come on then. But quiet though.'

So they crept upstairs. Ant had a spare mattress and a sleeping bag under his bed which Danny had slept on numerous times before. And, when Danny was finally tucked up, ready for bed, he told Ant that he needed his friendship now more than ever.

'You know I'd do anything for you, Dan,' Anthuan said. 'You're my mate and have been for as long as I can remember.'

'OK, thanks, dude. But will you lie for me?'

Anthuan paused. 'Why?'

'Because without your help, I'll never get to the Olympics. And I know you think my whole Olympic dream thing is crazy and that I'm slower than a cheese sandwich . . .'

'Hey, I'm so sorry about that.'

'Good. Then will you lie for me, Ant?'

'OK, I'm in.'

'Good man. That's agreed then,' Danny said. 'And if this all goes to plan, I'll get you two tickets to the Olympic 100-metres final. Which I'll be running in. Of course.'

'OK,' Anthuan said, still slightly perplexed. 'But what do I have to do?'

'You can start by going to school tomorrow and reporting that I'm off sick.'

'OK. And what will you be doing instead?'

'Training for the Olympics, of course.'

'Dan, you're crazy. You know that, don't you?'
'Maybe. But it feels great.'

The next morning, Anthuan began his career as Danny's lying accomplice. And Danny got on the bus for the Lee Valley Stadium. On the way, he checked his phone; right now, more than ever, he so badly wanted a text from Ricky. But no, nothing. He sighed and then resolved to forget about it; there were enough other issues on his mind already.

He knew it wasn't clever to miss school, but he had to. Otherwise there would be no Olympics. And he had to convince Spike that what he was planning was smart.

He paused outside the door of Spike's office and took a deep breath. He needed Spike on his side in this.

'What you doing here, Speedboy?' Spike asked, pulling the spectacles off his face in surprise, when Danny walked into his office.

'You told me, Spike, last night. Don't you remember?' Danny replied. 'You said that I have got to get "so, so, so much better". I think that's what you said. You might have said "so" four times, or maybe three. I don't know. But here I am.'

'Sorry, Dan.' Spike's voice sounded firm.

'What do you mean, sorry?'

'It's school time, Dan.'

'Yes, I know. That's why I'm here.'

'I don't get it. School comes first. And your A levels are round the corner. No debate.'

'I know. I know. But Spike, it's you who says I need to get so, so, so much better. And it's also you who always says we need a plan. And so, on this occasion, I've come up with a plan of my own.'

'Hmmm.' Spike sounded unconvinced.

'It's simple,' Danny replied. 'Today I'm missing school. I needed to see you. And I'm going to train harder today than you have ever seen before in your life. But from tomorrow I can't and I won't miss any more school. And I have to revise after school. So from tomorrow we're going to have to train first thing in the morning. Six thirty. And that's six thirty every morning.'

'You're crazy, Speedboy.'

'Funny that, Spike,' Danny said, laughing. 'Everyone seems to be saying that at the moment. Now, can we get down to work?'

'Sure thing, Speedboy. But first we have got some studying of our own to do.'

'What do you mean, Spike?'

'I'll show you.' And, with that, Spike swivelled round in his chair and started tapping on the keyboard of his PC. 'You may have beaten Uncle Carl and Uncle Jesse, but now you're going to have to beat the rest of the world. That's what I meant when I said you have got to get so, so much better. And I think I said "so" four times, not three. Anyway,

I've got two new targets for you to set your sights on. Come here, I'll show you.'

TARGET NUMBER ONE

As Danny sat down and looked over Spike's shoulder at his PC monitor, Spike explained himself. In Sheffield, Danny had got his PB down to 10.17 seconds. But the fastest British junior sprinter of all time was Dwain Chambers. When Chambers was a kid, he ran the 100 metres in 10.06 seconds. If Danny was to have any chance of running against seniors in the Olympics, then he would have to prove himself as the hottest junior first.

'Beat Chambers' junior record,' Spike said, 'and then people will sit up and take notice.'

TARGET NUMBER TWO

The mythical sub-10-second mark. Every good sprinter knew what the 10-second mark represented. If you wanted to be a world-class sprinter, you had to go under 10 seconds. If you hadn't run under 10 seconds – and Danny hadn't got close – then you just weren't in the running. Ten seconds. It was only a number, but, if you ran under 10 seconds, it meant that you were a contender; it meant that the other sprinters would respect you. It meant that you had a chance of winning one of the biggest prizes in the sport.

As Spike explained: every Olympic final since 1984 has been won in under 10 seconds. 'We haven't talked about it before, Danny, because I didn't think you were ready,' Spike said, 'but now's the time for you to break 10 seconds. I know you can do it. But here's what you've got to realize: if you can't go under 10 seconds, you might as well forget about the Olympics altogether.'

Danny frowned. He loved it when Spike got serious. And he loved the new challenges that Spike set him. But, though these were two awesome targets, he felt excited. He felt confident that he could do whatever Spike asked of him.

'Well, come on then, Spike,' he said, standing up. 'We better get down to work.'

'Too right, Speedboy!' Spike replied. 'You'd better be ready to die!'

Later that afternoon, Danny felt superb. Superb and exhausted at the same time. He felt well and truly, completely and utterly killed by Spike. They had worked and worked and worked. They had concentrated on Danny's start and they had not stopped practising it until they were convinced that Danny had improved it. In Sheffield the previous day, Danny's start had, by his own high standards, been poor. Even Jimmy Lewis had got a better start than he had. So he and Spike were intent on perfecting it. So they worked on that start, again and again. And then they did some general sprint work. And then they went back to work on his start again.

So Danny left the Lee Valley Stadium happy. Sixty-seven days to go. He wondered what Usain Bolt would have been doing in training that day. And he filled his mind with his Olympic dream all the way home.

'Hi, Dad,' he said as he walked in. He hadn't seen his father since he had walked out the previous night.

'Hi, son. Are you OK?' his father asked. 'You didn't come back last night. We were worried.'

'I'm sorry, Dad,' Danny answered. 'But I was in a foul mood. I went to stay at Ant's place. But I've had a long think about it all and you'll be pleased to hear that I've decided to put my A levels first.'

'Really?'

'Yes. Really. And I need you and Mum to know my new schedule. I'll be leaving at six every morning to do extra revision at Ant's house. So don't worry if you don't see much of me first thing.'

His father looked surprised but delighted. 'That's great, Dan,' he said.

And, every morning for the next two and a half

weeks, Danny intended to tell his parents that he was revising at Ant's house when actually he was training at Lee Valley.

This was the big lie. The biggest, fattest lie of Danny's life. And he never lied, he hated dishonesty and the last people in the world to whom Danny wanted to be dishonest were the parents he loved so much. Danny didn't like the arrangement, but it had to be done.

So this was his schedule: get up at 6 a.m. Training from 6.30–9 a.m. School at 9 a.m., revise for his exams and be home at 6 p.m. Then: work, bed, sleep. It was exhausting, totally draining and repeated every day.

At school, Danny resolved to hide away. He didn't want to lie to any more people than he had to. So he decided to do his best to talk to no one apart from Ant. Just train, work, bed, sleep. And lie every day. Every day was a lie, but it had to be.

But it was only for that short period of time. Because on 10 June Danny would run in the Olympic stadium in the British Olympic trials. And then his secret would be known to the whole world.

While Danny was busy training and working and lying, just one thing happened of note. A text came through from Ricky. It came totally out of the blue, totally unprompted, and it was just eight words long. Danny didn't really understand it or why it had come, but he didn't delete it and he started looking at it at night before he went to bed.

'Believe me, Dan,' it read, 'you must never stop running.'

★ 12 ★

COVER BLOWN

There were just sixty-three days to go when Danny left training in his usual rush. Train, bus, school – the schedule was tight and he would run from the track to the changing room, from the changing room to the bus and then from the bus stop to school. However, this time he left the changing room, school-bag over his shoulder, broke into a trot to get to the bus and then stopped. His mum was standing there. He felt embarrassed. *What on earth is she doing here?*

'Hi, Mum,' he said sheepishly.

'Hi, Dan,' she replied. She said it softly. There was no anger in her voice. He felt slightly relieved by that.

'How did you know, Mum?' he asked.

'It just didn't seem quite right,' she said, still in a soft, patient voice. 'I'd been thinking about it all week. I'd been worrying about you. I felt so sad for you after your dad and everything on Sunday, I barely slept that night. And I've been feeling sad for you ever since. But I still just didn't quite understand why you have to go to Ant's.'

'So did he tell you?'

'Ant? Of course not. He would never betray you. No, I just thought I'd find out for myself what was going on and so I got up early this morning and followed you.'

Danny didn't know what to do. He felt guilty, embarrassed. He didn't know what to say. He could hardly even look his mother in the eye. They stood there, the silence awkward, the only sound the traffic on the road.

'I'm sorry,' Danny said eventually, almost in a whisper. He could barely get the words out. He felt tears coming to his eyes. He never wanted to let his mother down. 'I'm so sorry.'

His mother opened her arms as if inviting Danny towards her and he accepted the invitation and hugged her tight. 'I'm so sorry,' he repeated.

'Don't be,' she said in a more sensible voice, pulling away.

'But what will Dad say?'

His mother smiled at him: 'He doesn't need to know.' Danny studied her face; he was bemused. 'Look,' she said, 'I understand your father's position. And I understand your position too. I think you're both right.' She paused and then started again. 'And I love you for your passion and the way you're pursuing your Olympic dream, and I want to support that. And I'm sure Ricky would agree.'

'Ricky?'

'I can't tell you for sure, but I suspect that Ricky would love to be where you are now.'

Danny stopped to take all this in. 'What if Dad finds out?'

'We'll deal with that if and when it's necessary.' She looked at her watch. 'Now, shouldn't you be getting off to school?'

Danny chuckled. 'It's not easy, all this.'

'I'm sure it isn't. Now that you've got me on your side, Dan, I need to know what I can do to help. Anything.'

'Oh, Mum!' Danny looked at her wide-eyed as if he couldn't believe his luck. 'You couldn't wash my running kit, could you?'

★ 13 ★

8 JUNE

Danny woke early. In fact, Danny had hardly been able to sleep. Today was the day, 8 June, the day of the British Olympic trials. Forty-nine days until the Games. Danny's legs felt twitchy in his bed. He looked at his clock. It was only half past five. He knew he needed to sleep. He knew that sleep would help. *But what can you do when you're lying in bed and all you can think about is the fact that later that day you're going to be running for your life in the new Olympic Stadium? Go back to sleep? No chance!*

He thought about Uncle Carl and Uncle Jesse and their achievements and what Spike always said about them. Be like Jesse Owens: noble and true to yourself. And be like Carl Lewis: strong, stronger than the others, don't care about the others or what they say because you are stronger than they are. And Danny thought to himself: *Wow! If I can achieve half of that, I'll be doing well.*

And then, when his clock showed that it was six o'clock, he slipped quietly out of his bed. Downstairs, his mother was waiting for him with a cup of coffee and the breakfast table all laid out. They were quiet and businesslike; she could sense Danny's nerves; she knew he didn't want to talk. Danny ate fast, kissed his mother on the cheek and left. It was quiet outside and already light. It would be a clear day; he liked that. And if it went well, it could be the greatest day of his life so far.

The Olympic trials are all about keeping your head. At least that was what Spike told Danny later that morning as they drove in his Ford Focus slowly through the traffic to the Olympic Stadium. After a race, Spike never tended to say that much; before it though, he couldn't stop talking.

'If you stay cool, Speedboy, you'll have the rest of them chasing you,' he said. Danny had that nervous feeling in his veins and said nothing. 'Got that, Dan?'

'Yup, got it, Spike.'

Spike then told him how the 100 metres would work. There would be four rounds of racing and eight runners in each heat. So, if Danny finished in the top four in his heat this morning, he would qualify for the quarter-finals in the afternoon. Then, again, if he finished in the top four in his quarter-final, he would be down to the last sixteen in the semi-finals early the following afternoon. And then, again, if he made it into the top four of his semi, he would be in the final that evening. There were three spots in the Olympic team and if you came first or second in the final, you were guaranteed one of the three places in the team.

OK, Spike, no problem, Danny thought to himself. *So you're telling me that the best sixty-four sprinters in the whole of the country have all come for this, and I've got to finish in the top two! It sounds impossible. It sounds like the hardest day of my life. It sounds as though my time would be best spent back at Newham Secondary working for my A levels. But I've come this far. No problem, Spike. I'll have a go.*

Danny was still mulling all this over as they drove in through the gates to the Olympic Park. Today was the biggest day of his running life, yet here he was, feeling like a tourist going on an adventure. Driving through those gates felt like he was walking through the front door to Buckingham Palace and sitting down to have tea with the Queen.

The funny thing was that he knew pretty much what it would all look like. He had spent long enough staring down at it all from his favourite spot in Bridge Road. He recognized perfectly well where he was. And yet, to see it all here and now, all glistening and new, it was like a huge, shiny Christmas present that had just been unwrapped.

They had to park the car and then get on a shuttle bus. The shuttle bus took them to the warm-up track. There was not just one track here in the Olympic Park but two: the one in the stadium for competition and the other outside for warming-up.

Danny could not hide a smile as he and Spike walked on to the track. It may only have been a place for the athletes to warm up, yet it was the newest, best track he had ever been on in his life. It was so new. The surface was so clean and so perfect.

He looked around. Some athletes were jogging round the track, some were practising their starts and some were running slowly, exaggerating their movements to stretch their muscles. And, on the side of the track, some were stretching and some were lying down having their muscles massaged. Everyone seemed serious. Not just the sprinters but the distance runners, the throwers and the jumpers too. Danny recognized some of them from having seen them on the television. For a moment, he just stood and stared, and then Spike interrupted his train of thought.

'Oi, Dan!' he said in a cold voice. 'You know what the one single difference between you and all the other athletes here is?'

'What's that, Spike?'

'Look at them. They're all concentrating; they're all totally focused on what they're doing. All they're thinking about is how to prepare for this race. And you? You're standing here as if you're sightseeing on holiday. Or watching animals in the zoo. C'mon, Dan. Sharpen up.'

That was exactly what Danny needed. *Pull yourself together, Dan*, he thought. There was an hour until his race. *Warm up slowly. Stretch. Listen to your iPod. Focus. Prepare.*

There were eight heats in the first round of the 100 metres and Danny was in the fifth. Runners would be called twenty minutes before their heat. He saw Jimmy Lewis walking out across the track, ready to run. Jimmy, he guessed, must have been in an earlier heat. Danny stretched some more. And then, finally, he heard the call: 'Heat Five, men's 100 metres. Please go through.'

Danny gathered his kit together. Spike was not allowed to accompany him any further. 'This is it, Speedboy!' Spike said. He put his hands on Danny's cheeks so Danny had to look him in the eye and take in his every word. 'Think of Carl and Jesse. Be strong and be true to yourself and then I'll meet you out here a little later and we can start thinking about the next race.'

Danny then followed the other runners out of the warm-up track and through a tunnel under the grandstands. Within minutes, they were walking out into the middle of the stadium. Danny stopped and gazed around him. It was beautiful. It was the biggest, most beautiful stadium he had ever seen. The stand towered high to his right. It was like being at the bottom of an enormous cereal bowl. There were not many spectators in the stands, but he looked around, imagining what it would be like in two months' time when the biggest show on earth, the Olympics, was here. It would be absolutely amazing.

He walked over to his lane and pulled off his track-suit bottoms. But he was still mesmerized. Here he was: in Bolt's Second Home. He looked over to the stand to see if he could spot Spike, but it was too big. He couldn't see him anywhere. Then he gazed to the side of the track, where he knew the medals would be presented during the Games. Then he looked up at the scoreboard; it looked like the biggest flat-screen TV he had seen in his life. He saw his name up there. It said: 'Daniel Powell, Lane Three'. *Pretty cool*, he thought. *Wouldn't mind a photograph of that.*

Around the startline, his fellow competitors were preparing themselves. Danny tried to catch their eye to see how they were, but they all avoided his gaze. So he looked out for Spike again and still couldn't see him. And then, suddenly, his thoughts were interrupted by the stadium announcer.

'On your marks.'

Danny rushed forward to the startline. He didn't feel quite ready. He crouched down, thrust his feet back into the blocks and prepared himself to go.

'Set!'

He looked down the track and focused on the finishing line.

Bang!

The gun went off and all eight runners burst

forward. Danny felt he had got a reasonable start but, as he hit full speed, he realized that he wasn't at the front. *There are four people ahead of me*, he thought. *Four! Dan, you have to hit the accelerator! You can't blow it now! Come on, Dan! This is not good. Pump! Pump your knees!*

At the halfway mark, it was tight. There was one man ahead and then Danny and four others, all side by side. *Pump it, Dan. Pump it!* He started to feel stronger. He started to feel good; he felt his knees pumping hard. But then they were through the line and, in the blur of the finish, he didn't have a clue where he had finished. Did he do enough? Was he in that top four?

He looked up at the scoreboard again. He was scared: scared that he hadn't done enough, scared that his Olympic dream was over.

The names then appeared in order. He wasn't first. He wasn't second. He was third. He was OK. He had qualified for the next round. *But that was too close*, he said to himself. *That was scarily close.*

He looked up at the scoreboard again to check his time. 10.19 seconds. *Not bad*, he thought. *But not nearly good enough.*

Outside, Danny met up with Spike again and they went together to get some lunch in the Athletes' Restaurant. But something was up. Spike didn't say anything. Not a word. Not 'well done' or 'that was close'. Nothing. He would hardly even look at Danny. He pushed some pasta round his plate with his fork as if he was lost in thought, but still said nothing.

Only when he had finished the last piece of pasta did he put down his knife and fork and look up at Danny. 'Right!' he said quietly and commandingly. 'Shall we go home now then?'

'What do you mean, Spike?' Danny asked. 'I've got the quarter-finals in three hours.'

'What I mean,' Spike said, and Danny could clearly hear the anger in his voice, 'is that it seems we're wasting our time.'

'Why?'

'Because I'd rather be at home digging my garden than sitting here in the stands watching you run like that.'

'You didn't think I ran well?'

'Look, Dan, get serious. This is the seniors. It's not school sports day. This is the big time. I thought you were ready for it, but now I'm not so sure.' Spike paused. He started to talk louder and faster and with more rage in his voice. He picked up his fork and was pointing it at Danny's chest as if he was going to spike him with it. 'You want to know why you didn't run well? Because you walked into that stadium as if you were on a school outing. I was watching you. You didn't concentrate, you weren't focused and you were staring around at the stadium as if you'd seen a naked woman for the first time in your life. Dan, I wanted to shake you. When the announcer said, "On your marks," I was surprised you even heard it.'

Spike paused again. Danny said nothing. He knew that Spike was right. Spike sighed and then said, 'Look, Dan, I sat in the stands just now watching you and asking myself a question that I now want you to answer: why have we been getting up at six in the morning these last three weeks? What was it for?'

'Because I want to win the Olympics,' Danny replied nervously.

'Exactly,' Spike said. 'And somehow you still have a chance. But you were lucky because, if you run like that ever again, it's over. End of Olympics. You won't get a second chance. Just now you forgot every lesson I've ever taught you. But you've now got an opportunity to put all that right. Come on, Speedboy. Concentrate, focus, be true to yourself!'

And, with that, Spike opened his rucksack and pulled out the chessboard. 'Come on,' he said. 'Let's prepare for this race properly.'

Nearly three hours later, when Danny was walking into the Olympic Stadium for his quarter-final, he still had Spike's words ringing in his ears. *Come on, Speedboy. Concentrate, focus, be true to yourself!*

And this time he was determined to get it right. He didn't even look at the crowd. He didn't notice where Spike was sitting. He certainly didn't realize that Anthuan was there in the crowd, sitting next to his mother. And in the back of his mind he felt further reassured. Just after Spike had beaten him at chess, Danny had received another text from Ricky. Again, it came totally out of the blue. It just said 'Good luck' and Danny loved it.

He was in Lane Seven and he went straight over to his lane and stared down the track. *Now is your time, Dan*, he thought to himself. *Now you have to get it right.*

He then glanced over at the other runners. *They look scared*, he thought. And he realized that he wasn't scared at all and he realized that he had a familiar feeling in his veins, as if he had had an injection of warm blood into his body: it was confidence. He had got the confidence back. *You can do this, Dan, you know you can.*

'On your marks.'

This time Dan was ready. He crouched down in the starting position.

'Set!'

Dan looked down the track. He felt like a caged tiger, ready to spring.

Bang!

He was off like a rocket. *Good start, Dan*, he thought, *there's no one with you. Concentrate. Pump the knees.* Danny was ahead of the other runners immediately. At the 30-metre mark, he had a clear lead. *Concentrate, Dan.* At 50 metres, the lead remained. *Push it, Dan. Pump the knees.* At 80 metres, it was clear he was going to win. *Don't let up, Dan. Keep it going to the finish.* And, as he sped through the finishing line, he tumbled to the ground in utter exhaustion. He knew he had run well, there could be no doubt. Surely.

Dan swivelled round to look at the scoreboard. His name came up first. But, when he saw the time, he sprang to his feet in astonishment, as if he could not believe it. He had run 10.03 seconds. *A PB! A beautiful PB! Faster than Dwain Chambers! Faster than any young Briton has ever gone before! You beauty!*

Danny felt brilliant. He couldn't believe what he had just done. He stopped and allowed himself a minute to look at the stadium in which he had just run his fastest-ever time. And then he followed the other runners out of the stadium and back to the warm-up track. He struggled to contain his joy. *This is brilliant*, he thought. *I am absolutely loving it!*

★ 14 ★

OVERNIGHT FAME

'Danny! Danny!'

As Danny left the stadium, he heard his name being called. He turned round and two people were running towards him. One was a woman, about thirty years old; the other was a slightly older man wearing a suit and an open-collar shirt.

'Can we have a word?' they said, slightly out of breath, in unison.

'We just watched you run,' said the man. 'You were fantastic.' He put out a hand to shake Danny's. 'Hi. I'm Pete O'Byrne. I'm the athletics correspondent of *The Times*.'

'Jenny Nicholas from the *Daily Express*,' said the lady.

Again, almost in unison, they both took notepads out of their pockets and smiled encouragingly at him. They then started firing questions and Danny was still so excited he was delighted to answer them. The pair of them seemed decent enough so Danny chatted away.

They asked him all sorts of questions. Some were about sprinting and technique and the Olympics. And some were totally bizarre, like: what did you have for breakfast this morning? And: what music do you listen to? And: where do you live? How far away from the stadium? And: are you still at school? And: what A levels are you doing? And Pete and Jenny seemed genuinely interested in all Danny's answers.

He was almost finished when another couple of men with a TV camera arrived and also asked for an interview and he said yes to that too. But first, he said, he just wanted to ask Pete and Jenny, the journalists, a question of his own.

'Are you going to write about me in your newspapers?' he asked.

'Absolutely,' replied Jenny, smiling encouragingly. 'Danny, you're a great story. You could be the star of the Olympics and here you are, living only five minutes away.'

'Hmmm.' Danny's mind started spinning. 'When will it go in the papers?'

'Tomorrow,' she said. 'And good luck tomorrow too.'

By the time he got back to the warm-up track, Danny had given two more interviews, one to Radio 5 Live and one to another group of newspaper writers, three of them. He was a bit taken aback by it all and so he was happy to find Spike there waiting for him. He knew he could rely on Spike for a dose of cold reality.

'Fastest British junior of all time!' Spike said. He almost seemed happy. 'Now I've got two things to say to you, young man. One: well done, you proved that you can do this. And two: go home, forget about what you've done and think about tomorrow. What you've done today is now irrelevant, Dan. If you don't run well tomorrow, today counts for nothing. Got it? Nothing. Nothing at all. It's all about tomorrow, remember. So go on now, go home.'

And so Danny did what Spike told him. Except he didn't go home. He met up with Anthuan and went back to his house instead. That had always been the plan and after what had just happened in the Olympic Stadium, there was no way he was going to change it.

Back at Anthuan's, Danny had jobs to do. First: he had to ring his mum. That was hard; he didn't want to get emotional. You only get emotional at the end of a race and Danny felt as though he was still in the middle of one. But he had to agree with his mum how to tackle the second job on his list.

He always knew this second job was going to be hard, but there was no escaping it. So he borrowed some paper, sat down and wrote a letter to his father.

Dear Dad,

I cannot tell you how sorry I am, but I hope and pray that you'll forgive me. I've lied to you and I hate that. I've always been honest with you. I never want to have to lie again.

Today I ran in the Olympic trials. I promised you that I wouldn't but I did.

And for the last three weeks, when I've been getting up at six o'clock, it wasn't to go and revise for my A levels as I said it was. It was to go and train for this race.

I'm sorry. I lied. But I've had this Olympic dream and I couldn't let it go.

But I haven't let my A levels slip down the pan. I've worked hard. Very hard. I was just convinced that I could keep my A levels and my Olympic dream going side by side. I ran well today and I feel I've done well in my A levels so far too.

Please forgive me, Dad.

I'll come home tomorrow night to face the music, but now I need to concentrate on the Olympics. Today I broke the British junior record. Tomorrow I need to run the two best races of my life and I might then get to the Olympics.

I understand that you may be disappointed with me. Please don't be.

Please join me in my dream. Mum is with me. I'll let her explain. And don't be cross with her. If you're cross with anyone, it has to be with me. But I don't want you to be angry at all.

I enclose two tickets for tomorrow at the Olympic

Stadium. There's nothing that could help me prepare better
than knowing that you were there and supporting me.
    Love,
    Danny

Danny folded the letter and put two tickets in the
envelope. Anthuan promised to deliver the letter first
thing the next morning; he also insisted that Danny
take the bed that night. 'You're the champ, man,' he
said. 'I'll take the mattress on the floor.'

'Thanks, Ant, you're a great mate.'

'And you, Dan,' Anthuan said, laughing, 'are a lot
faster than a cheese sandwich.'

Danny slept well that night, much better than the
night before. By the time he woke up, Ant had
already got up and gone downstairs. And, when
Danny followed him down, it was to discover that
life had changed somewhat. He was no longer just
a kid with a dream. He was a kid who was famous.

'Your secret's out now, Dan,' Ant said, a huge grin
on his face. 'I've already seen your face on Sky Sports
News. Your hair looks dead weird. You should
remember to do your hair before you go on the telly
next time!'

'Very funny, Ant!'

'But here,' Ant said, 'look at these. I went out to
drop off that letter earlier and I got these on the way
back.'

Ant pointed to the newspapers on the kitchen table. He had bought every newspaper in the shop and as Dan started flicking through the back pages, it became clear that they had all written about him. Every single one. *The Times* had his picture on the back page with the caption: 'Could this be Danny, champion of the world?'

Danny's heart started beating fast. Wow! He picked up the *Daily Express*, flicked in six pages from the back and there he was again, the headline: 'Local boy done very good.' Then the *Sun*: 'Danny, the Olympic super-kid.' The *Daily Mirror*: 'New kid on the Olympic block.' The *Daily Telegraph*: 'Local boy living the Olympic dream.'

He went on through the papers, reading and rereading them. He noticed from the results that Jimmy Lewis had got through to the semi-finals as well, but Jimmy barely got a mention. Everything was about *him*. The stories all seemed to concentrate on the fact that he was so young, that he was the new British junior record-holder and the fact that he lived little more than a kilometre from the Olympic Park. Some said he lived 'a stone's throw' from the Olympic Park; he could never throw a stone that far, but he figured that that wasn't really the point. Some called him 'the kid from nowhere'. Some said he was 'about to shock the world'. He liked the sound of that in particular.

But there was one element that appeared in every

story. Every single newspaper made the point that he had taken time out of his A-level schedule to run in the Olympics. They called him the 'A-grade Olympic student'; they said that he had gone 'from the exam hall to the Olympic stadium' and that he had 'passed yesterday's exam on the track with flying colours'. They even named his school, Newham Secondary. And some named the headmaster, Vernon McCaffrey. *Oh no*, thought Danny, *Mr McCaffrey didn't even know I was running today.*

An hour later, as Danny left Ant's house to meet up with Spike again, he realized that he felt funny. Not sick or anything. Not nervous. He just had this empty feeling in the pit of his stomach. It came from reading all those newspapers and it was very, very uncomfortable.

★ 15 ★

THE TRIALS, PART 1

Spike could tell that something was up. The moment he saw Danny, he knew. On race days, Danny was normally full of chat and he would walk around with his head held high, as if he was ready to take on the world. Today he was quiet, he seemed distracted and he kept his head down. They played chess and Danny was rubbish. He wouldn't concentrate at all. He lost in less than fifteen minutes.

Down at the warm-up track, Danny was going through the motions, warming up and stretching, but it was hard for him to concentrate because so many other athletes seemed to be paying him so much attention. Some just stared; some came up and shook his hand and said 'Congratulations'. Some joked to him: 'G'morning, superstar!' or 'Good luck with the exams!' And the occasional comment here and there was just plain nasty: 'It's all over now, sonny! I should get back to your homework!' said one. Another said: 'Enjoy the fame, kid, because you'll be forgotten about tomorrow.'

Danny didn't exactly warm to the spiteful comments but, more than anything, it just felt weird to be the centre of attention. Who were all these people? He recognized a few faces, but he hadn't spoken to them before. The only one he knew was Jimmy Lewis. Thank goodness for Jimmy – a familiar face. He sat and talked to Jimmy briefly and even though they were in the same semi-final, they wished each other luck. And then it was back to being the centre of attention again.

About an hour before his race, Spike put an arm round Danny and led him out of the warm-up track for a walk.

'It feels different today, doesn't it, Dan?' he said, but he didn't wait for an answer. 'I remember when it felt different for me. I was twenty-one, it was the European Championships in Athens and I was all over the newspapers too.'

'But you'd won a bronze medal, Spike. I've won nothing.'

'That doesn't matter, Dan. What matters is that you understand why you feel the way you do. Do you feel as though you want to hide, or run away, or as if you want to be sick, or scream out loud? Is that how you feel, Dan?'

'Sure is.'

'Well, that's how I felt too.' Spike then stopped walking and turned to Danny, talking really seriously. 'So here's the important bit, Dan. The bit that you really must understand. Here's the truth. The simple reason for you feeling funny is because you are good, really good: the best kid Britain's ever had. That's official, right? The complicated reason is this. Suddenly, everyone knows you're good: the other athletes, the newspaper people, the people who read the newspapers. They all know it because you showed them yesterday. And they all expect you to be good now, so they're all going to stare at you and watch you. That's what happens when you're good, Dan. Everyone watches. Now you've got two choices. Choice one: you can follow your feelings, run away if you want to and hide. You want to do that?'

'Not really.'

'Good. Well, this is choice number two. Every time you see someone looking, every time they make a comment, or stare, or if they're rude to you, or whatever – every time that happens, you have to tell yourself this: it's because I'm good. Now that can be very powerful, Dan. How many people, do you think, stared at you today or spoke to you who have never stared or spoken to you before?'

Danny shrugged his shoulders. 'I don't know. Maybe fifty, maybe eighty.'

'Good. Now that's fifty or eighty people telling you "you're good". Wow, Dan! I'd love to have that many people tell me I'm good. When someone tells you you're good, Dan, how does that make you feel?'

'I like it. It makes me feel strong.'

'Exactly. Well, you should feel strong fifty or eighty times over. You can go into this semi-final feeling stronger than you've ever felt before. Got it?'

'So these are your choices, Dan. And I want to know which one it's going to be. Are you going to take choice one, and hide or run away? Or choice two, and feel eighty times stronger? And I tell you: this is what Uncle Carl and Uncle Jesse were all about. How strong are you? Because those two were more choice two than any other sprinters that ever lived. So which is it going to be, Speedboy?'

Danny was quiet for a moment and then a smile crept over his face. 'Come on, Spike. That's the easiest question I've ever had in my life. I'll take option two.'

'Good man, Dan,' Spike said. 'You're sounding more like your uncles every day.'

Fifty minutes later, Danny was inside the Olympic Stadium, staring down the track, focusing hard. The crowd was far bigger today, it was almost a fully packed stadium, but he didn't even notice. He thought about what Spike had said and he felt strong, fifty or eighty times over. He didn't feel nervous and he could no longer feel that uncomfortable emptiness in the pit of his stomach. Instead, he felt that reassuring warmth in his arms and in his legs, that fantastic feeling of confidence.

His was Lane Five. Jimmy Lewis was Lane Two.

He recognized two of the other runners, in Lanes Three and Four. Deon Francis, in Lane Four, had been to the last Olympics. Tyrone Small in Lane Three had run for Great Britain many times and Danny had watched him on the TV. But he didn't think they looked scary. Neither of them. They looked normal. They each glanced his way a couple of times. *Are they telling me I'm good?* Danny thought to himself. *Now concentrate. Hard. Work your start. Make this your best start ever. Finish in the top four in this race and you'll be in the final.*

Bang!

The gun blasted. Danny reacted dynamite fast: it was as if he had pulled the trigger of the gun himself. Legs pumping. *Stay low at the start, pump the legs, drive hard in those first few strides. I'm ahead,* Danny thought. *I've got the start of my life. Concentrate. Keep your eyes fixed down your lane as if you're staring down a tunnel.*

At 50 metres, Danny was ahead. Clearly so. He felt that brilliant, flying, weightless sensation, as if his feet were barely having to make contact with the ground. Jimmy Lewis was back, hardly in the race. But Francis and Small were fast, clawing back Danny's lead. He could almost feel Francis next to him. *High knees, focus, straight ahead.*

At 80 metres, Danny was still ahead. Just. *Keep strong. Don't stop. Time your dip.* It's crucial in tight races to dip at the right time, to stretch forward your head and shoulders just as you're breaking the line. It was the difference between success and failure. Danny dipped. The crowd seemed to roar as he broke the line. *I've got it*, he thought. *I'm sure I've got it.*

He let his body tumble to the ground. As he hit the ground, he felt a very slight twinge at the back of his right leg, just above the knee, but he was too caught up in the moment to stop to think about it. He turned to read the scoreboard. It read: 'ist, Daniel Powell.' And then the time flashed up: 9.99 seconds.

9.99 seconds! 9.99! 9.99! Danny leaped immediately to his feet and punched the air. Once, twice, three times. *9.99 seconds! The mythical sub-10 club!* He could not believe it. He rubbed the back of his right leg. He hardly felt it, but it was as if he had brushed a stinging nettle.

And then Jimmy Lewis was at his side. Jimmy hugged him hard. 'How d'you go, Jimmy?' Danny asked.

'I didn't make it, Dan,' he replied. 'But forget about me. You were awesome. You were totally, completely awesome. Congratulations!'

The other runners all shook his hand, one by one. It was as if he was royalty; he'd never felt like this before. Tyrone Small clenched his hand tight and said, 'You're the man!'

Tyrone Small said that! Danny thought. *A guy I've watched and admired on TV!*

The last to shake his hand was Deon Francis.

'Sub-10, mate, well done!' he said. 'Welcome to the club.'

'Thanks,' Danny replied. But then another thought suddenly came into his head. *Is my dad here?* He scanned the crowd, but even if his parents were there, he didn't know where they would be sitting. And there were simply too many people in the crowd. It was impossible to tell. *Did they see me? Has Dad forgiven me?*

Danny waved to the crowd. But really he was waving to his mum and dad, whether they were there or not. *One more race*, he thought to himself. *Just go away now and focus on one more race.*

Danny walked away from the track. He felt great. He switched on his phone and there was a text, another one from Ricky. Just two words this time.

Nice one.

Danny liked that. He liked that a lot. Almost immediately, his phone beeped again. It was another text; another one from Ricky.

Now do it again.

★ 16 ★

THE TRIALS, PART 2

Between the semi-final and the final, there were three and a half hours to wait. But the story had changed even more. Yesterday he was a complete unknown; this morning he was the new kid on the block and now, suddenly, Danny Powell was the favourite to win. His time of 9.99 seconds was the fastest of the two semi-finals and up in the stand where the journalists were sitting, the discussion was all about him. Him and him alone: 'He's improving with every round!' 'How much faster can he go?' 'Can he keep it going?' 'Will the pressure get to him?' 'And what about Francis?' 'Francis nearly caught him!' 'Francis won't let that happen again!'

But Danny was not aware of any of this. Danny was with Spike, sitting in the Athletes' Restaurant playing chess.

First chess, then the iPod, then the warm-up track. Then the final. It was amazing how fast time could pass. Danny felt relaxed. He glanced around occasionally. He wanted to see: were people looking at him? They were. And now it made him feel strong. Just one more race, a top two finish and he would be going to the Olympics.

This time Danny was Lane Four. Francis was in Lane Five. And in Lane Three was the winner of the other semi-final, Max Donne. Donne was good. Danny knew Donne was good. But he didn't mind. He felt strong and he felt that warm blanket of confidence wrap itself round him.

He focused. He looked down the track and thought about his start, the power thrust, knees high, speed.

'On your marks.'

The stadium suddenly went silent.

'Set.'

Think of the start, Dan, then drive. Start and drive.

Bang!

Danny's reactions were lightning fast again. *Drive, drive the legs.* He had the lead early, but Francis was with him, and Donne too. *Focus, drive, pump high with the knees.* He felt Francis on his right; he knew Francis was edging ahead.

Pump, come on, pump it, pump it! And then suddenly, he felt a shooting pain down the back of his right leg. 'Aaaah!' He heard a scream of pain and realized it was his own. It felt like he had been shot by a bullet. Suddenly, he was hopping on his left leg. The pain was excruciating. Like a heat rush charging through his thigh muscle. He couldn't run any more. He saw Francis and Donne disappear away from him. He clutched the back of his leg. It was throbbing with pain. He was halfway down the track. He fell to the floor. It was over. The Olympic dream. Gone.

And there had been no shooting; there was no bullet and no blood. Of course there wasn't. Danny knew the feeling. He realized immediately what had happened. His muscle had torn; the physical stress of the last race had been too great. The muscle at the back of his thigh: the hamstring. It was a straight-forward injury. And here he was, lying in the middle of the track in the Olympic Stadium. His dream over. It was too much and he couldn't stop the tears. They just came, streaming down his face. Too much. The Olympics. All over. He sobbed and sobbed and he couldn't stop himself.

Francis? Donne? He didn't know who had won. All he knew was that his right leg felt as though it was on fire. And that the dream – the dream was gone. And that he simply couldn't stop crying.

The tears wouldn't stop. But it wasn't the pain. The pain was bad, but he wasn't crying because he was hurt. He was crying because his life had been all about a dream and now that dream was over.

The next voice he heard was reassuring and famil-iar. 'It's all right, Dan!' it said. Dan looked up and saw his father. He had come to watch after all! He must have jumped over the fencing at the side of the stands to get to him. 'It's all right, Dan,' he repeated again and again.

Dan let his dad haul him back up to his feet. 'I'm sorry, Dad, I'm so sorry,' he said.

'Don't be, Dan, don't be,' he replied. 'I'm so proud of you. So very proud.'

His dad draped Dan's right arm round his neck so he could support him and then they started to walk. Slowly, with Dan hopping on his left leg, the tears still dripping from his face, they started to move. They went all the way down Lane Four and, as they reached the finish line, the crowd rose to their feet and applauded.

'Listen to that,' his dad said. He stopped momentarily with Danny still leaning heavily on him. 'Look around, Dan. Listen. Listen to the applause. That's for you.'

★ 17 ★

INJURED HERO

Two days later, Danny was back at Newham Secondary. His intention was to carry on with school life and A levels as normal, but normality, it seemed, was now officially impossible. Anyone who hadn't heard of Danny Powell before the weekend now knew his story. The teachers, the school kids, everyone.

They knew exactly who he was, how fast he had run, how he had missed school on Friday in order to compete in the trials and how he had cried in his father's arms on Saturday. They knew it because the Sunday morning newspapers had written even more about him than the papers the previous day. And for those very few students who had somehow missed the news through the papers, the TV, Facebook, Twitter, the radio or the endless round of phone text gossip, when they got to school on Monday morning to find a small band of journalists waiting at the gates, it was obvious that something pretty unusual had occurred.

When Danny had arrived for school that morning, hobbling along on crutches, the press cameras clicked away as if he was a film star. And a little later, Mr McCaffrey, the headmaster, was outside giving interviews. Mr McCaffrey, it seemed, was not remotely unhappy with Danny; in fact, Mr McCaffrey appeared to rather like the idea of getting his own name in the newspapers too.

The Sunday papers had already changed the story. On Saturday Danny had been written about as 'the Olympic super-kid', but on Sunday he had become instead the 'brave local hero'. Almost every newspaper commented on the fact that he had cried in his father's arms and Danny was a bit gutted about that. The *Mail on Sunday* and the *Sunday Mirror* had both said that the tears were 'the tears of a brave man', but nevertheless Danny couldn't help feeling that crying hadn't been the coolest part of the whole adventure.

He also wondered about Ricky. No word from him at all. He had got those texts after his semi-final, but nothing thereafter. Why not? He so wanted Ricky back, back home, back with him, back as a brother and a friend. But this was just peculiar. He thought about texting Ricky the result of that final race, the same way that he always texted him his results, but that would simply have been strange. Ricky had surely watched it. *What on earth*, he wondered, *would Ricky think if I texted him the result of a race that has been plastered over every single national newspaper?*

Pretty much whenever he was around the school gates now, Danny was surrounded by other boys and girls in the school, some of whom he hardly knew, all of them wanting to ask questions about the Olympics. And the funny thing was this. Only four weeks ago, when Danny had said he wanted to run in the Olympics, he had been made to feel that it was a preposterous idea, stupid. 'Dream on, Danny!' was the general reaction. But now that he was hobbling around on crutches and the whole dream was officially over, no one seemed to think it was so stupid any more. In fact, most people seemed to think it was a great idea and they told him so.

'You'll be fit for the Olympics, won't you, Dan?' was the kind of question he found himself answering twenty times a day. 'How long till the leg's better, Dan?' 'You can do it, Dan.' 'Can we come and watch you in the Olympics, Dan?'

It was all very supportive, but a little frustrating as he found himself having to explain, over and over again, the sad circumstances. He was injured and it would take the hamstring an estimated four weeks to heal. But, even if he was fit by the time the Olympics started, the point was that he had missed his chance. He needed to finish first or second in the trials to get into the British Olympic team and he hadn't. He had finished eighth. Deon Francis and Max Donne were going to run in the Olympics and he wasn't. It was as simple and annoying as that.

And it was strange, but, as Danny explained all this over and over again, he somehow felt that he couldn't just dole out a barrage of non-stop miserable news. Even though he himself was the victim in all this, he felt he needed to cheer people up. So he would finish by saying: 'Never mind, I'll be back in four years' time. Don't you worry.'

And that seemed to work for pretty much everyone apart from himself. Danny tried to put on a brave face. It was cool that the newspapers had written so many positive stories about him and he didn't mind the fact that everyone at school now wanted to talk to him, even if it was a little hard to concentrate on his A levels.

There had been other good things to come from the whole affair too: his father had forgiven him, completely and utterly. In fact, because of what had happened with his dad running on to the track, he had sort of shared the spotlight with Danny. The journalists had wanted to talk to his father too, so Danny had felt as if they were in it together. And his parents looked after him at home as if he was a young boy again. His mum brought him breakfast in bed. He liked that. He might have been eighteen years old, but what he felt he needed was a great, big, long cuddle and that was what he was getting.

Yet deep down, he couldn't stop feeling sorry for himself. During those endless hours of revision, his mind kept on wandering back to the Olympic Stadium. *9.99 seconds! Sub-10 seconds! Welcome to the club!*

And then he would start to wonder: what if? *What if I hadn't been injured? How fast could I have gone? How fast will they go when the Olympics are in town? And how fast will Usain Bolt be? Would I, could I have beaten Usain Bolt?* All these questions were totally useless, an utter waste of time, but Danny couldn't stop them coming, especially when he was sitting at a desk with a history book open in front of him.

Yet, as the week wore on, the drama of the previous weekend seemed to fade a little. Exams became his life, not the Olympics. And the other school kids stopped asking him when he would be fit and running again.

On Wednesday lunchtime, he walked out of the exam hall after a really horrible business studies exam, tossing over in his mind all the mistakes he had made and the answers he had got wrong, and the first person he saw was Jess. She was sitting outside waiting to go in.

'Politics,' she explained. 'I can't stand politics!'

'When do your exams finish?' he asked.

'Friday,' she said.

'Me too.' Danny paused. 'So, do you want to go to a party on Friday night to celebrate? A load of us are going round to Ant's house. Should be quite fun.'

Jess frowned and looked confused. 'But I didn't think you ever went out, Danny?'

Danny chuckled. 'Yeah, I guess you're right there. Normally I don't. But normally I'm not on crutches.

Normally I'm trying to be an athlete. Now I'm just trying to walk without my right leg killing me.'

Jess laughed. 'Ah, you brave soldier, you! But that's so sweet of you to ask. Friday night sounds great.'

Danny hobbled off. He liked the idea of Friday night: a normal life, relaxing, having fun with friends. And not having to be an Olympian any more.

Friday afternoon and the end of exams could not come fast enough. Danny had two exams left: business studies on Thursday morning and, after lunch on Friday, a sports science theory exam. And then he was free: A levels over, a night to celebrate.

Thursday came and went and it wasn't too stressful. *I did OK*, he thought, *not great, but OK*. And he was confident about the sports science. For Danny, that was probably the easiest exam of the lot.

At two o'clock on Friday after lunch, Danny stood outside the exam hall, waiting with the other students for their last exam. It felt to Danny as if he was reaching another finishing line. At 4.30 p.m., he would walk out of the exam hall for the last time in his life.

Just as they were about to go in though, his phone buzzed in his pocket. It was a text message from Spike:

Don't give up yet, Speedboy. There's still a chance. Ring me.

Danny couldn't ring before the exam; there simply wasn't time. And for the next two hours, while he sat there writing about sports science theory, he tried desperately not to think about Spike's text, forcing himself to concentrate on the exam in front of him. It wasn't easy. But, the minute it was over, he hobbled on his crutches to a quiet corner outside the exam hall and made the phone call.

'Spike, it's me. What's up?'

'There's still a chance, Dan. That's what's up.'

'I don't understand, Spike,' Danny replied, trying not to get overexcited. 'I'm injured and I didn't make the team. How can there be a chance?'

Spike then explained. He had been phoned that morning by Charles Perryman, the head coach at UK Athletics. It was Perryman's job to pick the Olympic team. Perryman had said that he didn't want to give up on Danny, that he thought Danny's performance at the weekend was so good that they had to try everything they could to get him in the team. There were three places in the team for the 100 metres: one would go to Deon Francis, one to Max Donne and the third was for Perryman to decide. Perryman could pick who he wanted and the man he wanted was Danny.

Danny's heart started pounding as Spike told him all this. 'But I still don't get it, Spike,' he said. 'I'm injured. I'm on crutches. I am, right now, undoubtedly slower than a cheese sandwich.'

'I know, I know,' Spike answered. 'It's not going to be easy. In fact, I don't want to get your hopes up at all. But this is the deal. A hamstring injury like yours should take four weeks to heal. It's already had a week so, three weeks from now, it should be OK. That will leave you just three and a half weeks until the first round of the Olympics 100 metres. Now three and a half weeks isn't going to be long enough to get you up to full speed. You need four weeks or a month. So this is what Perryman has told me. He said that he'll keep that third place in the team open for you. In two weeks' time, he wants to see you. He's going to come down to Lee Valley to watch you run. And, if you can convince him you're fit, you'll be in the team. How does that sound?'

'I don't get it,' Danny replied.

'What don't you get?'

'My hamstring needs another three weeks. But Perryman wants to see me running in two. How am I going to manage that?'

'Ah, yes. That's the other bit that needs explaining. This man Perryman, he really seems to like you, Dan. He's made some arrangements.'

'What arrangements?' Danny was getting more intrigued and more confused.

'Well, I first need to check. You've finished your exams now, haven't you?'

'Yes, Spike.'

'Good.'

'And I'm just about to go out celebrating.'

'No, you're not, Speedboy.'

'What do you mean?'

'Do you still want to run in the Olympics?'

'Come on, Spike, you know I do.'

'Good. Well, go straight home, pack your bag for the weekend and I'll be round to pick you up in an hour. Oh, and grab your passport as well. We're going to Sweden.'

★ 18 ★

CRAZY SCIENCE

By eight o'clock that night, Danny and Spike were sitting on a plane bound for Stockholm. By five past eight, on this, the forty-second day before the Games, Spike was snoring loudly and Danny was left to his own thoughts, trying to ignore the snorting coach next to him, peering out of the window at the country they were leaving behind and contemplating what now lay ahead.

They were going to see the most famous sports doctor in the world. For most injured sportsmen, that would be good news. Managing to get an appointment with Dr Kris Gerndt meant you had a pretty good chance of getting better pretty fast. His nickname was Kris the Cure. Sportsmen and women came from all over the world to see him and almost all of them seemed to say that he was a miracle-worker. For years, Kris the Cure had been healing the injuries of tennis players, golfers, rugby players, footballers, the lot. And Danny knew that he was very lucky to see Kris the Cure. This Charles

Perryman guy had done him a massive favour by arranging it.

But there was a small problem. Indeed, if Danny had been able to, he would have run a mile from Dr Gerndt. Because Dr Gerndt's technique involved needles and injections – lots of them. And Danny hated needles.

He had never forgotten the time that Ricky had a tetanus jab. When they were still young teenagers, they were training together one day in West Ham Park and, after beating Danny – as always – over a short sprint, Ricky had thrown himself on to the grass and spiked his hand on a rusty nail that was sticking out of the ground. It was not the bloody gash in Ricky's hand that Danny couldn't look at; he was fine with blood. It was the injection the doctor gave Ricky in his arm. Danny couldn't even watch, so how could Ricky just sit there and take it – without even flinching?

This was what was going through his mind as he listened to Spike snoring. In his sports science A level he had done a special project on sports injuries. He could for instance give you, off the top of his head, his Top Five Weirdest Sports Injuries.

1. Dave Beasant, who played goalkeeper for England, once dropped a bottle of salad cream on his foot, severed the tendon in his big toe and couldn't play for two months.
2. Sammy Sosa, a famous baseball player in

America, once pulled the muscles in his back when he sneezed.

3. Sam Torrance, a Scottish golfer, couldn't stop himself sleepwalking and, one night, he was sleepwalking in a hotel and injured himself when he walked into a flowerpot.

4. David James, another England goalkeeper, once pulled a muscle in his back when reaching for the TV controls.

5. Rio Ferdinand, the Manchester United and England player, once injured the tendon behind his knee merely by having his feet up on a coffee table to watch the TV.

There was also a fairly interesting list of weird medicines and therapies that sportspeople used and Danny had studied those for his A level project as well. He had heard of athletes in China drinking turtle blood! The trouble was that Dr Gerndt's methods seemed the weirdest of the lot. What Dr Gerndt did was inject people's injuries with some really strange substances. Some of the stuff he injected came from calves' blood! And some came from the comb on the head of a cockerel! How on earth Dr Gerndt ever came up with all these crazy substances Danny had no idea. And why did he need so many needles? That was weird.

All Danny knew for sure was that if he was to have any chance of getting fit for the Olympics, he needed Kris the Cure badly. He had been booked in for two days in Kris the Cure's clinic. Kris the Cure was to be his torturer and, hopefully, his saviour too.

The next morning, bright and early, Spike and Danny were sitting in the waiting room in Gerndt's clinic. Danny gasped in awe at the photographs on the wall. They each showed Dr Gerndt with the various famous sportspeople he had worked with. Danny didn't realize that he had treated so many!

So he was feeling a little better when the man in all the pictures came in. Dr Gerndt high-fived Danny and then Spike. He was oldish, probably about sixty-five, and his hair was grey and lank, but he seemed full of energy.

'So you are the new young superstar?' he said in English, but with a strong Swedish accent.

Danny liked that. 'Well, I was hoping to be,' he replied, gesturing at his right leg. 'Until *this* let me down.'

'Well, we must make you better,' the doctor said. He said it as if it would be easy. Danny liked that too. 'I have a ticket for the London Olympics, for the final of the men's 100 metres. That is always my favourite moment in the Games. And, when I spoke to my friend Mr Perryman yesterday, he said that I would very much enjoy watching young Mr Danny Powell running that day.'

Danny nodded. He was a bit embarrassed to hear that he had been talked about in this way.

'So come on, Mr Powell,' the doctor said, gesturing with his hands. 'We need to get to work on you.'

And that was where it began. They went into Dr Gerndt's office and Gerndt started asking Danny questions: how did the right leg feel when he injured it? Where exactly was the pain? Did it feel hot or cold? How did it feel now?

Then Danny was asked to lie down on a therapy table and Gerndt put his hands on his leg, poking it in certain places. At first he was gentle, but then not. Gerndt talked to himself as he was doing this, muttering away, but always in English, as if he was talking to Danny's injured hamstring: 'Interesting, interesting. Good. Oh yes, yes. How's that feel? Ah. OK. OK. Oh dear. Oh, poor you. Yes, yes. Now I understand. Right, well, off we go then.'

And, after that, he took Danny into another room that looked like a space-age science laboratory and was full of large electrical instruments and computer screens. 'This is where we really discover what has happened in your leg,' Gerndt said. 'We have to find out everything about it; we have to get to know it as if it is our best friend.'

What followed was baffling. Gerndt wanted to have as close a look as possible at the troublesome hamstring so he took pictures of it, three types of scanned photographs using three different pieces of his space-age apparatus. This involved shooting X-rays through Danny's body, then supersonic sound waves and then magnetic waves. Cool. At least that was how it sounded when Gerndt explained what he was doing. Danny, however, didn't feel a thing.

An hour later, Gerndt had studied the pictures and was sitting back down in front of Danny and Spike with a rather different expression on his face. He didn't look so confident now and he frowned.

'Look, Danny,' he said. 'I have some bad news and some good news. The bad news comes first. Your hamstring is not so good. It is worse than I had expected. The muscles are quite badly strained. Normally I would say, "Forget it". Normally I would tell you that you need to mend your body and you should not run again for two or three months. That is the bad news.'

Gerndt paused, as if he was thinking, and then he finally smiled. 'Ah, yes. You want the good news, yes? Yes. OK. *Now* is not normal. *Now* we have to think about the Olympics. I have my ticket to the 100 metres – remember? – and I want to see you run. And I think you want to run too, yes, Danny? OK, so we have to do something special, to give you some magic. And we have to hope the magic works. But what is good, Danny, is that you have a healthy young body, and healthy young bodies mend more quickly. So . . .' He paused again as if he had forgotten what he was going to say. 'In order to help the hamstring muscles with the healing process, I am going to inject . . .'

It was at that point that Danny fainted. He had been waiting nervously all morning to hear that word, or to see the flashing point of a syringe, and at the very mention of the word 'inject', he collapsed in his chair. He regained consciousness within a couple of seconds and opened his eyes to see Spike and Gerndt both laughing uproariously at him.

So there was to be no sympathy there. Danny would have to face two days of injections. Into his hamstring Gerndt would be injecting a liquid extracted from fourteen different plants, among them daisies, marigolds and deadly nightshade, a flower that got its name because the ancient Romans used it as a poison. But Gerndt didn't tell Danny that last bit. He felt Danny had heard enough already.

Indeed, Danny did feel like a punchbag. Suffering from Gerndt's injections was bad enough, but almost worse was the news on his phone which he had left switched off until the treatment was finished.

There were a series of texts from Anthuan and Jess:

Where are you?

We're waiting for you.

Come on!

What's happened to you?

Giving up on you now.

Hope you're still coming round to my house later.

As Danny read the texts, it was as though Gerndt had now injected him with guilt. *How could I be so stupid?* he asked himself. *How could I forget to tell them?*

Then finally, the next morning, Anthuan had written simply:

What happened to you last night? I thought we were mates . . .

★ 19 ★

THE LONG WAIT

Danny had always thought that there could be nothing better in the world than being an athlete. Now he had arrived at a different conclusion: there was nothing worse in the world than being an injured athlete.

Or maybe there was. Maybe there was nothing worse than being an injured athlete and having your father fuss all over you. Since the end of A levels, Danny's dad had completely changed his tune. While his mum was lovely and caring and always looking after him, his father seemed to become the Prime Minister of fitness. He was continually checking that Danny had done every exercise he was given, checking his nutrition was right, checking that the treatment and the care he was getting was spot on. Danny started getting five, six, sometimes seven texts a day from him, every one of them checking up on him.

And this actually made him laugh. It was lovely feeling that his dad was by his side, his number-one supporter. If only he got the same from Ricky who had become strangely silent again.

Since surviving his two days of torture in Stockholm, Danny now had a new occupation: waiting. Waiting for his hamstring to mend. Waiting for the two weeks to pass to see if his Olympic dream was dead or alive. And those two weeks took so long to pass; Danny sometimes found himself staring at the second hand of his watch and wondering why it wouldn't move a little faster.

He went on the Internet to see what other sportsmen did when they were injured. Michael Owen occupied his time by buying racehorses. *Nice idea, Michael*, Danny thought, *but I'm still dependent on my dad for pocket money! I can barely afford a goldfish, let alone a horse!* Jonny Wilkinson had filled his time by learning French and teaching himself the piano. *Nice idea, Jonny, but I've just done my A levels. There's no room in my head for any more learning right now.*

Yet it wasn't actually as if Danny was bored or had nothing to do. In fact, he discovered that being injured was a very busy, full-time affair. When he got home from Stockholm, he was told he could have a day to rest and that he was then expected to travel up to Sheffield where he would spend a week at the English Institute of Sport. This, it turned out, had also been arranged by Charles Perryman.

And after Sheffield, he was allowed home, but he was nevertheless expected to spend every day at the

Olympic Medical Institute in north London. And that had been organized by Charles Perryman too.

The English Institute of Sport was a massive, modern sports complex and it had hotel accommodation so Danny could sleep there too. The Olympic Medical Institute was not so massive, not so shiny and new, and was attached to a hospital. But the reason he was sent to both places was because some of the best sports doctors in the country worked inside them.

Every day, Danny was put through a different schedule. A lot of it involved heavy massage on his leg. Sometimes he was put in the 'recovery pool', a shallow swimming pool that he had to wade up and down in to strengthen the hamstring muscles. A lot of the time was spent in the gym keeping the other parts of his body fit. And at the end of every day, when Danny was utterly exhausted, one of the sports doctors would have to write a report and send it by email to Charles Perryman to tell him how well Danny was progressing.

The big question was this: was his injury mending fast enough? Would he pass his fitness test?

But Danny had other questions on his mind too, like: how had he been so stupid and selfish not to think about his friends? He knew and accepted that being a professional athlete required him to be very dedicated, but he had never considered that it would turn him into a selfish or thoughtless person.

He had rung Anthuan from Stockholm and explained what had happened. And Anthuan had called him an idiot and many names much worse than that, but Anthuan also understood what had happened and he said he was happy for Danny that the Olympic dream was suddenly alive again.

Jess seemed happy to forgive him too. 'Don't worry, Dan,' her text read. 'Keep chasing your Olympic dream. You so deserve it.'

He knew, too, that Jess was right: he had only one priority in his life right now and it was the hamstring. Could it mend fast enough?

The newspapers seemed to enjoy asking the same question too. Every two or three days, it seemed, there would be a small story about him. 'Danny back on track' was the headline one day in the *Daily Express*. The next day the *Daily Mail* had a story saying 'Powell stuck in slow recovery'. As the day of his fitness test approached, the newspapers seemed to write more about him. 'Big doubts for Danny deadline day' was one headline on the same day that another paper's headline was 'Perryman positive for Powell'.

Danny wondered where all these stories came from and which ones were true and which ones weren't. But what he knew for sure was that, as the fortnight wore on, his leg was slowly improving. He was delighted when the day came when he could throw his crutches away. And, a couple of days later, he felt he could walk without feeling any lingering pain from the injury. What a boost to his hopes that was! But, while he could clearly feel that his body was on the mend, the question remained: was it mending fast enough?

Eventually, the day arrived. The day of the test. Danny awoke early and he felt more nervous than he had before any of his A level exams. He felt sick, but only through nervousness, and that didn't matter. What mattered was his leg. In fact, what really mattered was Perryman.

★ 20 ★
THE TEST

Charles Perryman was an impressive man. He wore a suit and was fifty-three years old though he looked more like thirty-five. In fact, he looked as if he could probably pass the fitness test and run in the Olympics himself.

But he impressed Danny because of the way Spike was behaving. Spike was quiet, pleasant and polite around him – and Spike wasn't usually quiet or pleasant or polite at all. And Danny also noticed that Spike didn't swear once in front of Perryman – and Spike usually swore a lot. In fact, Spike offered to make Perryman a coffee and when Perryman said, 'No thanks,' he then offered to make him a cup of tea. And it was normally the case that Spike expected other people to make the coffee for him.

They were sitting in Spike's office at the Lee Valley Stadium, chatting. It was a dark, grey morning and cold, and rain was hammering down on the roof. Danny felt more nervous than he had ever done in his life. Perryman had come, as promised, to oversee

Danny's fitness test; Danny just wanted to get on with it all.

But Perryman just seemed content to chat. He talked about how excited he was that the Olympic Games were coming to London. He talked about the athletes in his team and who he thought might win medals for Great Britain. 'Just imagine winning an Olympic medal here, in London, at the London Olympics, in front of a British crowd,' he said dreamily. 'That would surely be the best thing any British athlete could ever hope to achieve.'

That didn't make all this standing around waiting any easier. *Can't we just get out there and get it done?* Danny thought.

'Now, Danny,' Perryman said, 'how much faster do you think you could run?'

Danny was slightly surprised by the question. 'I'm not really sure yet, Mr Perryman,' he replied. 'I've gone under ten seconds already, so I'm hoping to go a lot lower.'

'Good. What do you think of your chances of beating Usain Bolt?' he asked.

That question surprised Danny even more, but he could only give an honest answer. 'I don't wish to sound cocky, Mr Perryman,' he said. 'But I've been training all year to beat him. And I wouldn't have trained so hard if I didn't think there was a chance.'

Perryman narrowed his eyes, looking at Danny as

if he was studying him closely. 'Good. Good,' he said. 'And would you like that chance, Danny?'

'Yes, Mr Perryman, you know I would,' Danny replied.

'Good. Well, you've got it then.'

'Pardon?' said Danny, totally confused. 'What did you say?'

'I said, "You've got it then,"' Perryman said, smiling. 'You're in the team. You're going to the Olympics!'

Danny looked at Spike and then back at Perryman, and then at Spike and then at Perryman again. Spike looked shocked. Perryman was grinning broadly. *Was this some kind of a joke?* 'But Mr Perryman, I thought, I thought . . .' Danny was now stammering. 'What about the fitness test? I haven't done it. I thought that's what you'd come here for.'

'No, Danny,' Perryman replied. 'I came here to tell you that you've passed the test already. I've been checking your progress every day since you got back from Stockholm. I've been speaking to your doctors and sports scientists and physiotherapists every evening and I've now got more data and analysis in my laptop about you and your right hamstring than I have on anyone else in my entire squad. Danny, I know more about your hamstring than you will ever know. So I'm not going to make you kill yourself out on the track now. I'm not sure it'd do you any good and you don't need to anyway. Because, even though you didn't know it, you've been kind of taking this test every day for a fortnight now.

'The thing is, Danny, I've had to learn about you fast. To pick you for the Great Britain team in the Olympics, I needed to know what you were like. Were you worthy of a place in the team? Would you do your country proud? Could you, at eighteen years old, really come to the biggest sporting event on earth and do a good job? And not be too scared? And so I haven't just been speaking to all these doctors about your hamstring, Danny, I've been talking to them about you. What are you like? And you know what? I now know how hard you have worked, Danny. I know that you have shown dedication. I know the answers to all the questions are yes. Yes, Danny, you would do your country proud. So I have been desperate to pick you for the team. I just needed your hamstring to come through the test too.

'And finally, last night, I spent another hour on the phone with the sports scientists at the Olympic Medical Institute and up at Sheffield. And we all agree that your hamstring will hold up. In fact, you'll do better than that, much, much better than that. In fact, Danny, between you and me, you're not the only one who thinks you've got a chance against Usain Bolt. I do too.'

Perryman then held out his hand to Danny and added calmly: 'So, Danny Powell, welcome to the Great Britain Olympic team.'

Danny grabbed Perryman's hand and shook it hard. He was speechless, but not for long. 'Thank you, Mr Perryman,' he said. 'Thank you, thank you, thank you. Thank you so much.' He still hadn't let Perryman's hand go. 'I won't let you down,' he said breathlessly. 'You won't regret this, I promise you won't.' He then paused, finally let go of Perryman's hand and asked: 'But would you mind if I give my coach a hug?'

'I think you should do,' Perryman replied.

And so Spike and Danny hugged hard. And then they suddenly started screaming. In fact, together they screamed so loud that Gladys on reception heard it.

'Olympics!' they shouted. 'We're going to the Olympic Games! We're going to the Olympic Games!'

Five minutes later, Perryman had gone. Danny still felt as though he wanted to shout and scream. He wanted to tell the whole world. But instead, he sat quietly in Spike's office and fired off three quick texts and then a fourth, which was slightly longer.

Dear Dr Gerndt. Your magic worked. Thank you for being my magician. See you at the Games.

Ant. I passed. I'm going to the Games. Thank you for being my mate. When these Olympics are finally done, I hope to be able to show you the kind of friendship you've shown me.

Dad, Mum. I passed. I'm going to the Olympics. Thank you for your support. I hope so much to make you proud of me.

Ricky. Dunno how you are or what's going on in your life. But I've just made it into the British team for the Olympics. This is the dream we always talked about. I've got there. I hope you're happy. I'd love you to come down from Liverpool and share it with me.

★ 21 ★

FAME AGAIN

Here we go again. That was Danny's thought when he woke the next morning to find that he was the big story in all the papers again. It was just three weeks until the Olympics opened and it seemed that excitement about the Games was growing by the day. Olympic news and gossip dominated all the headlines and now Danny was back as the main story again.

It was dead weird to be famous like this, all of a sudden. When he walked down the street, people would say 'Congratulations!' or 'Good luck!' or 'Bring us back a medal, Danny!' And he liked that. That was fine.

He also liked being the local boy. Over the last few years, he had heard so many people in Stratford make funny comments about their borough, things like: 'Nothing interesting has ever happened in Stratford before. And now we've got the Olympics!' And now, just three weeks away, so many people seemed so proud, so happy that they would be welcoming the world right to their doorsteps. It seemed that the Olympics had made everyone feel like a group, a close community, because they all wanted the visitors from around the world who were coming to the Olympics to think that Stratford was a good place with good people.

And now these people had their own Olympian, Danny Powell, their own little superstar. Danny liked that. He liked the fact that he helped them feel that they had something to be proud of. Not only did they have their own Olympics, but they had their very own man to cheer for.

So that was the good bit about suddenly being famous. There were some funny parts to it too. Once a week since he collapsed injured during the trials, he had received a package through the post that was sent from the main offices in the Olympic Park. It contained letters, all of them sent to him. It seemed that people who wanted to write to him were putting his name on the envelope and then, below it, the address of the London Olympics – it was as if they thought he lived inside the Olympic Stadium!

That was strange enough. But these letters came from people from all over the country and some from other countries too, and they were all from people he had never met. They all said they were his fans and that he was their hero. Some letters came from girls who had put lots of kisses at the bottom of the letter. Some girls even included their photograph and phone number and asked him to give them a call.

Predictably, it was Anthuan who was most excited about all the fan mail. To be precise, Anthuan was excited about the female fan mail and he took it upon himself to write back to all Danny's female admirers on his behalf.

The bit that Danny didn't like about suddenly being famous were all the newspaper stories. That morning, after getting his place in the Olympic team, all the newspapers were discussing him. Almost every story about him said nice things – 'Well done, Danny', 'Three cheers for Danny!' That sort of thing. But they all went further than that.

They started asking questions about him and about what it would be like for him to be in the Olympic Games. Some newspapers said that there would be a lot of pressure on him to do well, maybe too much pressure. One newspaper wrote: 'The boy is only eighteen and his body has already broken down once on his brave march to the Olympics. Can we reasonably expect him to get to the finishing line still in one piece? Are we not asking too much of this courageous young man?'

Hmmm, Danny thought when he read that. *I'm not worried about that. Not worried at all.*

But there was something else, something that he did not find quite so easy to dismiss. On that first day of the trials, he had met those two journalists,

Pete O'Byrne, the guy from *The Times*, and Jenny Nicholas, from the *Daily Express*, and because he now knew their faces, he had started to read what they wrote. And today they both wrote about him and they both said pretty much the same thing.

In the *Daily Express* was:

Danny Powell is clearly the most exciting young athlete we have seen in this country for a number of years and his talent deserves admiration and support. However, it is a little crazy to believe that an eighteen-year-old is going to be an Olympic champion. It is plain and simple: he is too young. Yes, he is brilliant. Yes, he may become Olympic champion one day, in four years' time or eight perhaps. But not now. Boys of eighteen do not become Olympic sprint champions.

But what worried Danny even more was what he read in *The Times*. Pete O'Byrne had laid out lots of facts, all about the ages of sprinters at past Olympics, and they were not very friendly facts at all. Usain Bolt, when he won the 100 metres four years ago in the last Olympics, was five days short of his twenty-second birthday and the guys who finished second and third behind him were twenty-three and twenty-two years old. The guy who'd won the 100 metres in the previous Olympics, in Athens, had been twenty-two years old. And the guy who'd won four years before that, in Sydney, had been twenty-six.

When Carl Lewis first won the 100 metres, he was twenty-three.

This was what Pete O'Byrne wrote:

The history of athletics tells us that sprinters do not hit full speed until their early twenties. Bolt was unusual to have gone so fast at the age of twenty-one. When you look back at years and years of athletic performance, the evidence is not encouraging for the splendid Mr Powell. No one has been able to run faster than the rest of the world until they have reached their twenties. Certainly no one who is eighteen. Powell has already given us shocks and entertainment aplenty, but it would be the biggest shock of all if he was to push his eighteen-year-old body to achievements that no teenager has ever managed before. A teenage human body is not designed to do what Powell hopes to do. It sounds simplistic, but Powell is just not old enough to beat Usain Bolt.

Hmmm, Danny thought when he read it, *that wasn't really what I wanted to hear.*

★ 22 ★

HOW TO BEAT USAIN BOLT, PART 2

At training later that morning, Spike was in a furious mood. He was holding up a copy of *The Times*, shaking the newspaper in his hands and bawling at Danny. Danny had just made the mistake of telling Spike that he had seen the article and was slightly concerned about what he had read.

'You believe this?' Spike yelled. 'You mean to say you've read this and now you think you can't win? Danny! Come on!' Spike was shouting so loudly that Danny actually found himself edging backwards so that he was pinned against Spike's office wall. He could see the veins on the side of Spike's head bulging as the volume rose. 'Speedboy – what's happened to you? Yesterday you were singing and dancing because you'd been selected to run in the Olympics. And today you've read a couple of newspapers and you don't think you can win any more? Come on, Danny! Come on! Pull yourself together!'

Spike sat down in his chair and shook his head in dismay. Then he stood up again and then sat down.

Danny wasn't sure what to do, so he did the only thing he could think of and offered to get Spike a coffee.

Spike sighed loudly, shook his head again and then started talking, more slowly, more quietly, with his teeth closed, as if he was trying to contain his anger. 'No thanks, Dan. There is one thing you can do though. Leave the building now. Take a walk round the stadium and clear your head of the rubbish you've been reading. Just empty it all out so there's not a single word from *The Times* left infecting that sensitive little mind of yours. Walk once round the entire building and then come back here. I'll be waiting. And then we can get back to work. We've got a lot of work to do. We've got a man called Usain Bolt to beat, and it won't be easy.'

So Danny left Spike's office. He smiled to himself. He hadn't seen Spike in a rage like that for quite some time. When he saw that bulging vein on the side of his head, he thought Spike was about to explode. He knew that Spike would soon calm down – he always did. He just needed a bit of peace and quiet.

But Danny didn't walk round the building as Spike had instructed. That would have been absurd. He just went upstairs and said hello to Gladys on reception. He liked Gladys. She was always there, every day, always cheerful, always greeted Danny with a smile. They chatted for a while; Gladys told Danny about her son and daughter and how well they were doing at school. And, after five minutes, Danny excused himself, made Spike a coffee and took it downstairs to him.

Spike was staring at his computer screen and didn't look round at Danny. 'Enjoy your walk?' he asked.

'Yup. Just what I needed,' Danny replied. Spike couldn't see the smile on Danny's face. And the smile vanished the minute Spike swivelled round in his chair.

'Dan,' he said, quietly and seriously. 'I'm going to say this once and then we are moving on. Right?'

'Right.'

'You've forgotten about Uncle Carl. At least, that's how it seems to me. But you need to remember Uncle Carl now more than ever. If you worry about what other people are saying or thinking, you might as well not bother with the Olympics. Carl Lewis didn't care what the rest of the world said about him. In fact, he took great pleasure in ignoring them. He believed in himself and he loved proving everyone wrong. Again and again and again. Now it's your turn, Dan. Prove everyone wrong. Believe in yourself. Like Carl, Dan. Just like Uncle Carl.'

'I know, Spike. You're right.'

'Good,' Spike said. 'Because we've got work to do. There's less than a month until the Olympics

100-metres final. Now pull up a seat. I need to explain to you how you're going to win it.'

Spike started tapping the keys on his keyboard and Danny pulled his chair in closer so he could see. Up on the screen was a page entitled 'The Plan'. And under 'The Plan' was another headline: 'How to beat Usain Bolt'. Danny liked the sound of this. The next thirty minutes would be very important. Danny knew that and so he listened hard.

Usain Bolt, Spike explained, is the best 100-metres runner of all time. No argument about that. Everyone knows it. But he has a weakness. It's only a small weakness; in fact, it is so small that it has never bothered him in the past. But if anyone is going to beat him, they have to make the most of it. 'And,' Spike said slowly, 'it's all about reaction times.'

The ability of a sprinter to react to the starting gun in a 100-metres race is crucial. The quicker you react, the better. In other words, if you react fast to the bang of the gun, you'll get a fast start.

Technology is so advanced nowadays that, in top races, they sometimes use a recording device that can measure the sprinters' reaction times. In other words, it measures the time between the starting gun firing and the sprinters starting to move. Their reactions, obviously, are astonishingly fast. The quickest sprinters can react in not much more than a tenth of a second; the average reaction time of the best in the world is around one and a half tenths of a second.

'Now look at this,' Spike said as he tapped his keyboard again so that a new set of numbers appeared on the screen. 'These are the reaction times of the eight runners in the final of the men's 100 metres in the Beijing Olympics four years ago. What do you see?'

1. Richard Thompson, 0.133 seconds
2. Walter Dix, 0.133 seconds
3. Asafa Powell, 0.134 seconds
4. Darvis Patton, 0.142 seconds
5. Marc Burns, 0.145 seconds
6. Michael Frater, 0.147 seconds
7. Usain Bolt, 0.165 seconds
8. Churandy Martina, 0.169 seconds

Danny looked at the reaction times and focused particularly on Bolt's. *Very interesting, very surprising too.* Bolt's reaction time in the final was 0.165 seconds. That made him the second slowest in the race.

'You see what I'm saying?' Spike asked.

'I think I do,' Danny replied.

'Good. Well, you'd better look at this then, too.' Spike then pulled up some more numbers on to his screen. They were more reaction times from Beijing, this time from Bolt's 100-metres semi-final, and Danny leaned in to get a closer look. Bolt's reaction time in the semi was 0.161 seconds. That made him the third slowest starter in his semi-final.

Danny had never realized this before. *Bolt is a slow starter!* he thought. *Spike really does have a point. Bolt's reaction times are slow.*

Spike leaned back in his chair and raised his eyebrows at Danny. 'What do you think, Speedboy – interesting, eh?'

Danny paused. 'Yes,' he said. But the tone of his voice suggested that he clearly wasn't certain. 'The bit I don't get is this, Spike.' He paused again, as if he was trying to assemble his thoughts. 'I see what you're saying: he doesn't have the greatest of starts. And that should really hurt him. But it doesn't, does it? He may have had a bad start, but he still won the gold. He still broke the world record. If he's still going to destroy everyone else, what good is a slow start to us?'

'Good question, Dan,' said Spike. 'And here's your answer. Bolt always wins because he's so relaxed, so confident. These other guys – they might have a better start than him, but they lose it so quickly. He's always caught them by the 20-metre mark. And once he's passed them, they'll never catch him. But I wonder: what if you put Bolt under pressure? What if you can keep your lead a little longer? He's never been under pressure because he's always been ahead. So we don't know what he's like under pressure. For the last four years, he's never been scared; no one has worried him. What if you got him scared? What if he suddenly thought: this isn't quite so easy any more? What if he started to worry: I might not win?

'Here's a fact, Dan: some people like pressure and most people hate it. Obvious, I know. But what if Bolt is like most people? What if he hates it? Then someone else might win the Olympic 100 metres instead. And who's that going to be, Dan? Who?'

Danny never gave an answer to Spike's question. He didn't need to and Spike didn't need to hear it. But Danny understood loud and clear what Spike was saying and he thought it was brilliant. What a plan! What a coach!

The next two weeks were given over to Spike's plan. Danny spent his nights dreaming about the Olympics and his days at Lee Valley working on his start. He hardly saw anyone else or thought about anything else.

At the track, Spike worked his plan brilliantly. He went out and bought the newest and most expensive set of blocks he could find, which also contained a timing device to record the runner's reaction time. That way, Spike and Danny could work endlessly on Danny's reaction time. The first day Danny did fifty-five timed starts; the next day sixty-seven; the day after that forty-eight. And the thrill that Danny derived from this was huge because he saw his average reaction time get better and better and better.

Alongside the track, Spike had put up a large sign saying: 'Bolt's Beijing reaction time: 0.165 seconds'. And so for every recorded start that Danny did in training, the target was to beat 0.165 seconds. And then to get faster and faster and faster. And the ultimate goal was to have a reaction time faster than everyone in that Beijing final.

Danny was a fast starter anyway. His first start was 0.159 seconds. But after the first day of intense practice, he was down to 0.150 seconds. By the end of a week, his average reaction time was 0.142 seconds and, in the second week, it was coming down further.

On the last day of 'block work', Spike gave Danny a challenge. 'I want to see three starts under 0.135 seconds, OK, Dan? Three in a row,' he said. 'And once you've done that, I think you'll be ready for the Olympics.'

Immediately, Dan got to work. His first three start times were 0.133 seconds, then 0.134 seconds and then 0.129 seconds.

'OK, Speedboy,' Spike said. 'You now know.'

'I know what, Spike?' Danny replied, a little confused.

'You now know what it takes to beat Bolt. Now off you go. You're as ready now as you'll ever be.'

★ 23 ★

THE UNFORGETTABLE OLYMPICS

The Olympics are not just about running; they are not just about trying to get medals or trying to beat Usain Bolt. At least this was what Danny was quickly learning. As the days passed and the Olympic 100 metres got closer and closer, there were four episodes in Danny's life that he thought he would never forget.

UNFORGETTABLE OLYMPIC EPISODE ONE

Here is the weird thing about the Olympics: the amount of free stuff you get. A week before the Games, Danny was told to report to the British Olympic Association's headquarters in Central London to be given his team kit. He knew he needed a team suit and a team tracksuit and a couple of Team GB running vests, but he had no idea that he would be leaving with a pile of free clothes, shoes and stuff so big that even Santa would not get it all in his sack.

What Danny had never realized was that, by qualifying for Team GB for the Olympics, he had earned himself five pairs of free Team GB pants. And he didn't just get one Team GB tracksuit, he got three. He got two pairs of Team GB wrap-around sunglasses. He got four Team GB baseball caps. He got a pair of Team GB trainers and three pairs of Team GB shoelaces. That was to say nothing of his ten Team GB polo shirts, the seven pairs of Team GB shorts and a Team GB umbrella. He decided he would give his Team GB box of chocolates to his mum and his Team GB cufflinks to his dad. He was just about to ask why he would need a pair of Team GB gloves in the middle of summer when he was also given a Team GB dressing gown, two pairs of Team GB pyjamas, a Team GB toothbrush and some Team GB toothpaste.

Danny had been intending to take all this home with him on the London Underground, but he realized that he had so much stuff that he had to take a taxi. On the way home, he texted Ant excitedly:

For being my mate, I've got a gift for you. I would like to present you with your very own pair of free Team GB slippers and a pot of Team GB hair wax.

UNFORGETTABLE OLYMPIC EPISODE TWO

The day before the Olympics were due to start, a week and a day before the athletics competition would begin, Danny moved into the Olympic Village. And he could not believe what he found there. In fact, the Olympic Village was so big that initially Danny found nothing; all he did was get lost.

The Olympic Village is where all the athletes and their coaches live during the Olympics. It can house around 5,000 people so it is less like a village and more like a small town. It is also a very exclusive place to go. Only Olympians are allowed in, no one else. There is a meeting zone near the entrance where friends and guests are allowed, but there is a limit. They cannot, for instance, go to the massive food hall where you can get everything from McDonald's to Norwegian pickled herring. And yes, to Danny's extreme delight, he realized that this was all free too, even the Norwegian herring.

Sometimes Danny had to pinch himself. Every day here, he felt partly like a kid and partly like a tourist. He wanted to say 'Hi' to everyone he recognized and at the same time he wanted to ask for their autograph. Instead, he kept on texting Anthuan:

In the food hall, Michael Phelps is sitting twenty metres away.

Or:

Just met Chris Hoy. What a great guy!

Or:

Did you know that the best-looking female athletes in the Olympics all seem to do the pole vault?

It was only because of the flags that Danny stopped getting lost. Almost every team from every country had its own apartment block and they would drape huge national flags out of their windows and over the apartment block walls. So Danny soon worked out that, to get to the Team GB apartment blocks, he had to go left out of the food hall, down past the Canadian block and then the Russian block, then right at Brazil, past Egypt and New Zealand then right at Morocco and there, on the apartment block in front of him, would be a cascade of Union Jack flags. He liked that; they made it feel like home.

Danny's room was in GB Block Two up on the fifth floor with most of the athletes. The swimmers were below him on the fourth floor and the cyclists were up above on the sixth. Danny's room was next to Deon Francis and Max Donne, all three of the 100-metre sprinters together in a mini-apartment, Flat 32, with a shared sitting-room area. This was great. Deon and Max were not his rivals any more as they had been in the trials the previous month. Now they were teammates, they supported each other, they encouraged each other and, after a while, they started joking around with each other.

Sometimes Planet Olympics seemed so weirdly

155

amazing that Danny had to pinch himself. *Remember why you're here*, he would say to himself. And then he would go to his room and reread the words on his bedroom wall. Because Spike, typical Spike, had printed off two pieces of paper and told Danny to stick them up and read them every day.

On one of them was a famous quote from Uncle Carl: 'My thoughts before a big race are usually pretty simple. I tell myself: "Get out of the blocks, run your race, stay relaxed. If you run your race, you'll win. Channel your energy. Focus."' Danny liked that and he kept replaying it in his mind. *Focus, Danny. Focus.*

The other quote was from Uncle Jesse and it was short but very sweet: 'One chance is all you need.' Deon and Max liked that one in particular, so much so that they started saying it themselves too. 'One chance, guys,' Deon would say in the mornings at training. 'That's all we need.'

There was something else that Deon said, something that Danny really liked. The three of them were relaxing in their flat one afternoon after training, chatting about the Games ahead, when Deon sat forward in his chair, as if he had just had an idea. 'I've got a good feeling about these Games,' he said. 'I really, truly believe that one of us three is going home with a medal.'

Max then looked at Danny and nodded his head in approval and, in turn, Danny looked at Deon. 'Sounds very good to me, Deon,' he said.

'Cool,' said Deon. 'Let's shake on it then.'

So the three of them clasped hands in a triple handshake. 'To us,' they said together. 'To a medal for Flat 32. To a beautiful shiny medal for a British sprinter.'

UNFÓRGETTABLE OLYMPIC EPISODE THREE

Like much of what happened at the Olympic Games, Danny had watched the Opening Ceremony on TV. He had seen it, thought it looked amazing. And here he was now, actually taking part in it.

At the Opening Ceremony of the Games, there are fireworks and dancing and singing. In fact, it is one long celebration. And, at the very end, the Olympians – the competitors in all the teams from all around the world – join in. They march into the stadium, team by team, in alphabetical order, led in by a member of their team carrying their Olympic flag. Thousands and thousands of them. But, because Great Britain were the hosts, they did not march in alphabetical order. Instead, they marched in last. And they got an astonishing reception from the crowd.

Danny walked into the stadium with Deon on his right and Max on his left, and the noise was so great he could barely hear himself think. As they waved to the crowd, the crowd waved back. In fact, the crowd shrieked back. And Danny could not stop smiling. He turned to Deon and started talking, but Deon couldn't hear so Danny shouted instead: 'I now understand why they call it the greatest show on earth!'

He also wondered what his parents would be thinking, watching on the television less than three kilometres away. He wondered what Ant would be thinking too so he texted him:

Feel like a rock star!

But there was one other thought that was playing on his mind. *Come on, Dan, enjoy it, enjoy it all you can. But remember, the next time you walk inside this stadium, it will be business. You're not here to wave, Dan, you're here to run.*

UNFORGETTABLE OLYMPIC EPISODE FOUR

As if Danny needed any reminder of why he was there, he got it four days later. He knew it was coming; he knew it would happen soon enough. In fact, he was a little surprised it hadn't happened earlier.

It was at breakfast in the Olympic Village. Half past nine. He was with Deon and Max as usual and they were walking over to a table to eat. And that was when Danny saw him, sitting at a table about thirty metres away; he was looking relaxed, chatting and laughing with his friends. In fact, he didn't look

particularly different from anyone else in the break-
fast room that morning. But it was him.
Unmistakably him. Usain Bolt. The man himself.
Here at the London 2012 Olympics.

Danny stood transfixed. He didn't want to move.
He wanted to stand there and watch. There he was,
the giant of Beijing. This was the man Danny had
watched and admired. And now he was the man
Danny had to beat.

The London Olympics, Danny knew, was the greatest experience of his life. But he also knew that no
matter how great the experience, life still ticked on.
He might be here at the Olympic Games, he might
be running for his country, he might be in the same
breakfast hall as his hero, Usain Bolt. Yet Ricky, his
brother, was still nowhere to be seen, nowhere to be
heard. Silent, absent, gone.

★ 24 ★

GOING FOR GOLD

As each day passed, the tension rose in GB Block Two, Flat 32. It grew little by little, so much so that Danny barely noticed. He knew that having Deon and Max with him was a godsend. They helped keep him calm. And, because they were each experiencing the same feelings of nervousness, they all understood how each other was feeling. But there was no doubt about it: as their big moment approached, the laughter started to die in Flat 32.

In fact, when they awoke on the morning of 4 August, they were all a little relieved. Here it was, their date with destiny. The moment they had been training all their lives for. The 100 metres of the London 2012 Olympics. The waiting was over.

The three of them breakfasted early, but they barely talked. They were serious, nervous; it was hard to make conversation. It was hard even to eat.

Danny saved his talking for his parents. He rang them at home, and he didn't know what to say, he just wanted to hear their voices. He just wanted to be reassured.

'You'll be brilliant,' his dad said. 'We are so proud of you. Whatever happens today and tomorrow, we are so proud.'

The three of them then headed to the warm-up track together to prepare. Danny was relieved to see Spike there waiting for him. Spike looked relaxed and that was what Danny needed. Because Danny still felt nervous and he didn't like that. Why hadn't the nerves gone? Where had that warm, reassuring confidence gone?

Danny tried to ignore the nerves. Instead, he got on with the job. He stretched, he jogged a little. He listened to his iPod. He tried to ignore the fact that, on the very same warm-up track, were another seventy-nine of the best sprinters in the whole of the world. Yes, Bolt was there. Bolt was pretty much the first man Danny saw when he arrived. Bolt looked huge, he looked awesome. *Stop it*, Danny thought to himself. *Ignore Bolt. Concentrate on yourself and not him.*

Just like in the trials, there would be three rounds of racing in order to reach the Olympic final and the competition would, of course, get harder and harder as you got through each round. The first round – the heats – they should be the easy ones. At least that is what Spike told him. 'Use the heats to find your feet,' he said. 'You feel nervous. Of course you do. It's the Olympics. Everyone feels nervous. You wouldn't be human if you didn't feel a bit like that. So go out into that stadium and get used to it. Get used to the crowd, get used to the tension. Focus, run well. And then come back here and we'll start talking about the next round – that's when the competition begins to get serious. But first – how about a game of chess?'

That sounded like a good plan to Danny.

There were ten heats and he would be going in Heat Three. He liked that: nice and early. Get it out of the way. And there was only one other name he recognized in his heat: Ryan van Zyl from South Africa, a powerful, tough runner who was brought up in safari country and told anyone who would listen that he only knew he was a decent runner when he was eighteen years old and successfully saved his life by running away from an angry, rampaging elephant.

Van Zyl was in Lane Six and Danny was in Lane Seven. And as Danny made his way to the stadium, he found himself thinking about that elephant; he also realized that he still felt nervous. And it was when he walked into the stadium that those nerves really hit him; he could feel his heart pumping. Every single seat in the entire stadium was full. And the crowd was shouting and screaming and cheering. And it was a noise like Danny had never heard before. Loud, ecstatic, excited.

Danny knew that, somewhere in here, his mother and father were watching him. And Ant was there too; he had come with Jess. But that didn't really help. Because there were so many thousands of people, Danny would never have seen them. And he shouldn't have been thinking about them anyway. He looked down at his vest; was his heart now beating so fast he could see his skin moving?

Come on, Dan, concentrate, he thought to himself. *Relax, remember what Spike said, this is the easy round.*

But it wasn't easy. They went down in their blocks, 'Set!', and then came the bang of the gun. But the bang was followed, within a split second, by a second bang. A false start.

Danny looked nervously around. *It wasn't me, was it?* He didn't think it was. What if it was? *I'm sure my start was good.*

There was a restlessness in the stadium as the runners and the crowd awaited the news. Who had false-started? Who was to have their entire Olympic dream wrecked by instant disqualification?

Next to him, Danny heard the throaty, hard tones of a South African. It was van Zyl, talking to him. 'You feeling scared, little boy?' he said. His accent was strong and sounded threatening, and Danny could see the flashing gold of his chain and, as if to match, the flashing gold of one of his canine teeth. Danny ignored him, but van Zyl didn't stop. 'Hey, little boy, I'm talking to you.'

Still Danny ignored him. He was not enjoying this. Not at all. 'Hey, little boy,' van Zyl said. 'I know you think it was you. You must be scared. Very scared. Do you want me to find your mummy?'

Still Danny ignored him. At least he tried to.

But van Zyl's creepy comments were interrupted by the stadium announcer. 'False start. Lane Four. Disqualification: Shinji Mirita of Japan.'

Danny stared at Mirita. He knew he shouldn't. He knew he was supposed to be concentrating on the race he was about to run. But Mirita looked as if his life had ended. He said nothing, did nothing, just looked around the stadium as if he was saying goodbye, and then walked backwards, a slow retreat from the Olympic Stadium, as if he couldn't bear to take his eyes off it.

But Danny was quickly shaken back to his senses. 'Lucky for you, little boy!' came the rasping whisper next to him.

He hated van Zyl. He wanted to win this race, but he was suddenly far more interested in beating the South African.

'On your marks.'

Danny went to his blocks. *Make sure you kick van Zyl's butt*, he said to himself.

'Set.'

He readied himself.

Bang!

Danny knew his start was poor. *But at least there was no false start.* He felt the runners on his left; he knew he was struggling; he knew van Zyl was comfortably ahead. *Come on, Dan!* Halfway and there was still some catching to do. Van Zyl was out of reach. *Come on, Dan. Stretch now.*

Danny dipped his head and shoulders forward at the finish. He knew he had run an appalling race. *Have I done it? Have I made the next round? Or have I blown it?* The whole race felt so close that he didn't have a clue.

He looked up at the scoreboard. Van Zyl had won in an easy 9.98 seconds. Then the scoreboard showed that the guy in Lane Two, from Ghana, was second. Danny waited for the third place result to come up. *Please let it be me! Please let it be me!*

And it was. Third place: Daniel Powell, 10.10 seconds. He was through to the next round.

'Hey, little boy!' Danny could hear van Zyl's throaty, South African voice behind him. 'You're too scared, little boy. These are the Olympic Games. You won't last another round.'

Once again, Danny didn't answer. But he couldn't help wondering if maybe van Zyl was right.

Spike was already at the warm-up track, waiting for him. *Thank God for Spike.* Danny felt he needed him more than ever. He knew that Spike would be furious.

He knew that Spike would tell him that he had run a lousy race. But he still needed some reassurance. He needed it badly.

But Spike wasn't furious. In fact, Spike wasn't angry at all. Spike was almost laughing. He was clearly chuckling to himself.

'What's so amusing, Spike?' Danny asked, completely mystified. 'I nearly screwed up the entire thing. I'm lucky to still be here in the Olympics. I was nervous, nervous as hell. And that van Zyl – what a lowlife! I let him get into my head. I let him bother me. Pretty much everything that could have gone wrong did go wrong, Spike, and you think that's funny?'

Spike paused to let Danny catch his breath and then he replied, slowly and warmly. 'Dan, I'm laughing because I'm glad. You're right. Everything you've just said is right. Yes, you did mess it up, big time. But you've also just told me why. You know perfectly well why. Because you were nervous. And because of that idiot van Zyl. I'm glad because if you understand why you messed it up, then you know perfectly well how to stop yourself doing it again.'

Danny looked at him perplexed.

'OK,' Spike said. 'Let's talk it through. How far did you run in there just now?'

'100 metres.'

'And is that any different to the distance you normally run?'

'No.'

'Good. So remember: it might be the Olympics, but everything else is the same. It's still 100 metres. You're still running in a straight line. There's nothing you are doing that is remotely different to anything you've done before. So forget that this is the Olympics. Just go out there and run the way you always have done. It's worked before and it'll work again.'

Danny nodded.

'And van Zyl?' Spike asked. 'C'mon, Speedboy! He was talking to you, right?'

'That's right, Spike.'

'And why? Why was he talking? Because he wanted to make friends? Why you and not the others?'

'I don't know, Spike,' Danny replied.

'Yes, you do, Dan. He's talking to you because he knows you're good. He's trying to unsettle you, Dan, because he's worried about you. Remember? But actually he's paying you a compliment. Bullies like van Zyl only target the competitors they're scared of. You need to remember that, Dan. Got it?' Danny nodded. 'Good. Now think about that and go out this afternoon and put it into action.'

And Danny then did exactly what Spike told him. In the second round in the afternoon, he ran a near-perfect race. He won in a time of 9.99 seconds. And he felt great.

And now he was in the Olympic semi-finals. The dream was still alive. More alive than ever.

And he also had a text on his phone. It was from Ricky.

Keep going. Just keep on going. Two more races. I know you can do this. But whatever happens, I cannot tell you how proud of you I am.

★ 25 ★

THE CLIMAX

Today was the big day. Yesterday had been a huge test, but today was what really counted. Deon and Max had both passed yesterday's test too. They were both still in the race, but Flat 32 that morning was almost silent as they each contemplated what was ahead of them.

They had the whole day to get through. The semi-finals were not until seven o'clock in the evening. If they finished in the top four, then they would be in the final. At half past nine.

Danny felt horrible, nervous, as though he was waiting for his own execution. He could not wait for this evening, to get it over and done with. And yet he realized that he felt scared of it too. And the wait seemed so slow. He looked at his watch so often he began to wonder if it had broken. *Why wasn't that minute hand moving any faster?*

Just before lunchtime, Charles Perryman came to Flat 32. He said that the Team GB website had crashed because so many fans had been posting 'good luck' messages to Danny, Deon and Max. He also said that he had intended to carry up the bag of fan mail that had arrived for them, but that it was too heavy. 'But personally,' he said, 'I just wanted to wish you luck. And don't forget, this is the Olympics. It's special, boys. Try and enjoy it.'

Enjoy it? Was he having a laugh? Danny actually knew Perryman was right. He knew that relaxation and enjoyment would be the key to a good performance, though it didn't help that when he saw Usain Bolt in the food hall at lunchtime, he was smiling and laughing with a couple of others from the Jamaican team. *What's so funny, Usain?* Danny wondered. *How can you be so relaxed? And why can't I laugh and joke around like you?*

After lunch, Flat 32 decided they needed a distraction. A movie. That would help pass the day. So they watched *Rocky*, the film starring Sylvester Stallone as a heavyweight boxer. But, even during the film, Danny couldn't let his mind be distracted. He couldn't enjoy it. He still kept on looking at his watch. *How long to go? How long to go? How long to go?*

So he went into his room. He felt he needed to be with Uncle Carl and Uncle Jesse. He read their comments on his wall. Uncle Carl: 'If you run your race, you'll win.' And Uncle Jesse: 'One chance is all you need.' He read them and then reread them over and again. They made him feel a little stronger. He wished that Carl and Jesse could be here now, but he knew too that they had done what he was about to do, and they had been alone too. And it was all right to be nervous. Wasn't Jesse nervous? Did he not swallow hard as he crouched down, waiting for the *Bang!* of the gun, waiting to claim his gold medal?

But no words could make Danny feel better than the text from Ricky. Danny reread it and discovered that there were twenty-four other texts on his phone, from friends, family, from other sprinters, one from Jimmy Lewis, one from Kris the Cure, there was even one from Mr McCaffrey, his old headmaster. And they were all full of support. And he read and reread the one from his father:

> Danny, I never thought you could do this. But I was wrong. A lot of other people – your school, your competitors, the newspapers – they never thought you could do this either. You proved them wrong too. You proved us all wrong. Keep on believing in yourself. Keep on proving us all wrong. You had a dream. You can now make that dream come true.

That made Danny want to cry. And then he read and reread one from Ant:

> Bring me back gold, my friend. I hear Bolt is so scared of you he has cancelled his order of cheese sandwiches.

That almost made him laugh. In fact, that was the closest Danny came to finding anything funny all day.

*

To his great relief, Danny was in the easier semi-final, the second one, with Deon. Max was in the first and, in that race, he had both Bolt and van Zyl to contend with. Bolt was looking magnificent. Van Zyl was tipped as one of the very few who had a chance of beating him.

But the warm-up track was beginning to resemble a fast-moving reality TV show with contestants being voted off at a frightening rate. Yesterday morning, there had been eighty of them. Now they were down to sixteen. And forty-five minutes later, they were down to eight. And Max didn't make it. He finished fifth. His Olympic dream was over.

But Danny and Deon survived. Danny ran 9.99 seconds again and he felt better, confident. He finished third with Deon second. And their semi-final had only just finished when Deon wrapped Danny in a huge hug. 'Remember what we talked about?' he said, bouncing on his feet, the adrenalin and excitement shooting through him. 'We're in the final. Can you believe it? We're in the Olympic final! But we've done nothing yet. Remember what we said: there's going to be a medal from Flat 32. It's you or me, Dan, you or me!'

'Or both of us!'

★ 26 ★

THE OLYMPIC FINAL

Danny sat on the warm-up track, iPod plugged in, trying to focus. There wasn't time for chess. He thought about Kris the Cure, he thought about his father and mother and Juanita, his father's mother. He thought about Spike. And about Charles Perryman. And Ricky. And Ant. He thought about all these people who would be watching in the stadium. All these people who had supported him. He wanted to perform for them. He wanted the medal. He wanted to beat Bolt.

Focus, Dan, focus. He thought about Uncle Carl: *Be strong, don't be scared.* And he thought about Uncle Jesse: *Be true to yourself.*

And then Spike reminded him where his mind should be. On the start. On his reaction time. On beating Bolt at the gun.

'What was Bolt's reaction time in Beijing, Dan?' Spike asked.

'0.165 seconds,' Danny replied.

'Exactly. And tell me, Speedboy: what sort of reaction time can we expect from you?'

'I'll settle for 0.13.'

'Excellent. Start well, Speedboy. And then think of Uncle Carl: if you run your race, you'll win.'

It was just then that Danny's phone bleeped to signify a text. He liked these pre-race texts. They made him feel good.

But this one, he saw, to his horror, was from no friend. 'I know you're scared, little boy,' it read. 'Go home. You don't belong here any more.'

Danny deleted the text immediately. Then he looked across the warm-up track and on the other side he saw van Zyl, grinning back mischievously. *How did he get my number?* Van Zyl looked delighted with himself. He even started laughing.

That's all I need, Danny thought. But to make matters worse, as they started the walk over to the stadium for the final, van Zyl appeared by his side, so close that Danny could smell the sweat on his body. Danny moved to his left, but van Zyl followed him.

'You can't run away now, little boy,' van Zyl said in a quiet, threatening whisper. 'I can tell you're scared. You're scared, aren't you?'

Danny put his headphones back on to shut out van Zyl. But even then he saw the South African grinning at him cruelly.

Rise above it, Dan, he said to himself. But he was struggling and he knew it. All of a sudden, he felt nervous again. *Where's that warm confidence gone?*

When they walked into the Olympic stadium, they

were greeted by the loudest roar Danny had ever heard in his life. Danny took one look up at the crowd and then swallowed a big, lumpy swallow, just like Uncle Jesse's. And then he composed himself. *C'mon, Dan. Think of your start. Think of your reaction time. Think of 0.13 seconds out of the blocks. Think of Uncle Carl. Run your race and you'll win.*

He was in Lane Seven, Bolt was Lane Four, Deon was Lane Five and van Zyl was Lane Six. Van Zyl next to him – that was not what Danny needed. He still felt nervous. He felt more alive, more on edge than ever. But still nervous. *Where's my confidence?*

And then he heard that low, rasping, South African accent next to him again. 'Hey, little boy, you poor thing, you must be absolutely terrified.'

'On your marks!'

Danny stepped forward and crouched down, jamming his feet back into the blocks. A hush suddenly fell upon the whole crowd. You could hear a pin drop.

'Set!'

Now was the moment he had been waiting his whole life for.

Bang!

Bang!

Two bangs. A false start. Van Zyl rounded on Danny immediately. His face wore that same cruel grin, the gold tooth sparkling at the side of his mouth.

Was it me? Was it me? The whole crowd was suddenly murmuring, waiting for the stadium announcement. Who had gone early? Who had false-started? Who was about to be slung out of the Olympic final? *Was it me? Was it me?* Danny didn't know. He wanted to, but he wasn't sure. He thought he had got a good start. He had been trying so hard for a good start. But was it too good? Had he gone early? *Was it me?*

He looked at his seven rivals. No one seemed sure who it was. Deon shrugged. Bolt didn't seem to care.

There was no announcement. The stadium announcer seemed to be taking an age to discover who had transgressed. This was so painful. Again, Danny scanned his seven rivals. They were beginning to look impatient. Who was it? *Was it me? Was it me?*

And then at last: 'False start, Lane Seven, Daniel Powell.'

★ 27 ★

IT'S ALL OVER

Danny did not know what to do. Probably every single spectator in the whole stadium was watching him, watching how he behaved when faced with this horrible, horrible humiliation. Danny stood stockstill for a second, feeling the pounding in his chest, harder and harder, feeling the tear ducts of his eyes desperate to let go. He wanted to cry. But he knew he could not cry with the TV cameras of the world watching his every move. So, in a fleeting moment, he decided to run for it. He wanted away. He wanted to be as far from the Olympics as fast as he could go.

So he turned and ran. He ran back down the tunnel and out of the stadium. He was still in his running spikes, but he didn't care. He had left behind his kit, his iPod, his phone, his trainers, his tracksuit, everything. But he didn't care. He didn't care about anything.

Even though he didn't know where he was going, he knew the route. He had spent so long gazing down at the Olympic Park from Bridge Road he knew the fastest way out of the Olympics, out of the stadium, right up the slope, over the small bridge, then left, past the velodrome and the aquatic centre.

Danny was half-sprinting, half-crying. Some passers-by didn't even register him. Others stopped and stared. He heard others commenting, as if confused: 'Isn't that the young runner . . .'

But he didn't stop. Not for anyone. He couldn't stop until he was on his own. Completely and utterly alone.

He turned right again to the main gate out of the Olympic Park. He was supposed to stop at the security gates, but he didn't; he ran straight past and then just kept on going.

The furthest a sprinter normally runs in one go is 400 metres. That is their limit. But Danny just kept on going, away from the park, up towards Bridge Road and then round the corner until he had run nearly three kilometres and had ended up in Widdin Street. Back outside his own home.

No key. Of course he had no key. You don't carry your house keys on you when you're in the final of the Olympics 100 metres. So he started running again. Up the road, round the back of the houses and down the alley. He clambered over the wall at the back of the small garden behind his house, retrieved the spare key from where it was always kept beneath a flowerpot and let himself in.

Only when he got upstairs to his room did he kick off his spikes. He threw himself down on his bed and then he finally allowed himself to cry. In fact, he sobbed. He sobbed loudly. He pumped tears into his pillow.

His mind remained fixed on that split second, that moment in the stadium when every single spectator was looking at him.

'False start, Lane Seven, Daniel Powell.' And with that it was over.

'False start, Lane Seven, Daniel Powell.' His dream was finished.

'False start, Lane Seven, Daniel Powell.' All that work. The years of training. The effort. All wasted. All completely wasted. Buried. Over. The Olympic dream was snuffed out.

The tears kept pouring from Danny's eyes. He didn't know for how long. He didn't know whether they stopped when he eventually fell asleep, or whether they stopped purely because there were no tears left to pour out. But some time later, probably around midnight, an hour and a half after the Olympic 100-metres final, Danny's Olympic pain was brought to an end by pure exhaustion.

The Olympics had been so tiring. Danny had been either on edge, or on a high, or just hopelessly over-excited for over a week, nearly two. And he didn't realize the toll that took on his body which was suddenly crying out for the opportunity to rest and recover. The sleep he fell into was deep. So deep that when his parents and Ricky eventually got home from the Olympic Stadium, they couldn't stir him.

And if he was dreaming, it certainly wasn't an Olympic dream any more.

★ 28 ★

FALSE START, LANE SEVEN

Danny woke late the next morning. It was just before eleven o'clock. It seemed strange to wake up in his room because he was used to waking up in Flat 32, but he realized, within a millisecond, where he was and why. The whole of the previous night came flooding back into his mind, washing over him and knocking him over like a tidal wave.

'False start, Lane Seven, Daniel Powell.' The words started drumming through his mind immediately.

'False start, Lane Seven, Daniel Powell.' He buried his head under the pillow.

What happened to me? How could I have let that happen? Why? Why did I false-start?

He dragged the curtain gently back so he could see outside. It was a grey day. And then it struck him: he didn't even know what had happened in the final. *Did Bolt win? Did the awful van Zyl get a medal? How did his mate Deon do? Oh, Deon.*

Danny hoped Deon had won a medal. But he also

realized that he didn't care. He didn't want to know. He didn't want to be a part of the Olympics any more.

'False start, Lane Seven, Daniel Powell.' As far as he was concerned, that was the end of it.

At midday, there was a knock at the door. It was Ricky. Ricky! Really, really Ricky. He smiled at Danny and gestured to the cup of tea in his hand.

'I'm sorry, Ricky,' Danny said.

'What are *you* apologising for?' he whispered back. 'You don't have to be sorry for anything.'

There was silence. There was probably no one else in the world that Danny would rather have seen than his brother, but still he felt uncomfortable.

'What are *you* doing here anyway?' he asked.

'I'm glad you asked,' Ricky replied, sitting on the side of Danny's bed. 'I just wanted to explain.'

'Explain what?'

'Where I've been? Why I disappeared. Because it kind of seems important now.'

Danny frowned at him. There was a brief silence. Why was Ricky talking to him about this now? What did this have to do with the idiot in Lane Seven?

Ricky took a deep breath and then started talking. 'You don't know how brilliant you are, Danny,' he said. He seemed to breathe a sigh of relief as he said it. 'I know you feel like hell. I know you hate yourself for your false start. But I cannot tell you how proud

I am of you. And I can hardly explain how jealous I am too.'

'Jealous?'

'Yes, jealous.'

'Why?'

'Because you've done what I wanted to do. I wanted to become a runner and I didn't. You did. I wanted to run in the Olympics and I didn't. You did. I had the same dream as you and I didn't follow it. I wasn't as brave as you, Dan. I did the sensible thing. The right thing. But it wasn't the brave thing.'

'What d'you mean, Rick?' Danny asked. 'You're going to graduate from university in a year's time. You're a super-soaraway success.'

'Maybe,' said Ricky, rolling his eyes. 'But I cannot tell you how many times I've sat in the library at Liverpool University wishing I was down at the training track with you and Spike. And I cannot tell you how many times I've wondered: what might I have achieved? Could I have got to the Olympics? How good could I have been if I'd pursued my dream?'

'Pretty hot, if you ask me,' replied Danny.

'Maybe,' replied Ricky. He let the silence return and then started talking again. 'But I'll never know, will I? And if you want to know why I went so weird on you, never talking, never texting, never being your friend, your brother: it was because I was jealous of you, Dan. Every time I knew that you were running, it made me jealous. I was scared of you being successful because every time you won another race, it would make me think that I could have been successful too.'

'That's stupid, Rick!'

'I know. I'm not very proud of myself. But then, this summer, it got ridiculous. You started doing so well, I couldn't be jealous any more, just amazed at every astonishing step you took. So I went from being jealous to being your number-one fan.'

'Well, why didn't you tell me?'

'I didn't want to butt in. You had enough going on. I thought it best to leave you alone.' He stopped, paused and then started again. 'But I can't leave you alone now, Dan, because I've been desperate to talk to you, to tell you two things.'

'What's that then?' Danny looked confused.

'Well, firstly, that I'm sorry I've behaved like an idiot. And, secondly, that you may not have won the Olympics last night, but you've won admiration around the world. You might feel rubbish inside, but you shouldn't, Dan. What you've done is amazing.'

'Thanks, Ricky,' said Danny. He held out his hand. Ricky took it and shook it firmly.

After a moment's silence, Ricky asked: 'How are you feeling?'

'Still worse than I've ever felt in my life,' Danny replied, though he managed a chuckle.

'Can I get you anything?'

'No thank you.'

'Will you come down for lunch soon?'

'No thanks.'

'You've got queues of people hoping to see you. And the phone's been going mad with people wanting to ask if you're OK. Do you want to see them, speak to them?'

'No. Not yet.'

'Dad?'

'Not yet.'

'Mum? Spike?'

'Not yet.'

'Ant? A rather nice looking girl called Jess?'

'No one yet. It's going to be a while before I can face the world again.'

Danny stayed in his bedroom for the rest of the day. He didn't eat or drink. He didn't talk to anyone. He slept a little. But most of all, he was replaying over and over in his mind the events of the night before. 'False start, Lane Seven, Daniel Powell.'

Only at around midnight, after he was sure that his family had all gone to bed, did Danny eventually get up. It was weird. He hated the Olympics and yet he still loved them. He never wanted to hear about the Olympics again, and yet he was desperate to find out what had happened in the 100-metres final. He knew that he couldn't avoid reality forever. So he went downstairs and made himself a sandwich. It was a cheese sandwich and he managed to chuckle to himself as he made it. Ant was right: Usain Bolt could indeed have eaten a cheese sandwich before Danny got to the finish. Because Danny never even got there.

Then Danny went through into the living room and turned on the TV. He had asked his father to record the 100-metres final – his final. And here it was.

He fast-forwarded through the beginning. He didn't want to watch himself being disqualified. He just wanted to watch the race.

So there they were: seven runners in the Olympic final when there should have been eight. And a gaping hole in Lane Seven. Bolt got a bad start. That made Danny smile. But then he caught the rest of the field. No surprises there. Bolt was brilliant, beautiful and strong with his trademark long strides. Again Bolt seemed strangely different from everyone else, as if the mechanics of his body had been put together differently.

The medals: gold to Bolt. It had to be, didn't it? Silver: Ryan van Zyl. Danny hated that. He despised van Zyl. Bronze: Deon Francis.

Deon! Bronze! For the first time in twenty-four hours, Danny felt a glimmer of real, genuine happiness. So Flat 32 did get its medal.

Danny knew he couldn't keep licking his wounds and feeling sorry for himself for very much longer.

The next day he was happy, though, to see Ant.

And he had a long chat with his father and mother. And Ricky kept close to him. Ricky seemed to understand best how he was feeling.

Everyone was lovely to him and full of support. And they all told him he had done so well. Danny himself still felt he was a failure and he would probably never stop feeling that way. But everyone else told him that they were proud, that it was a truly astonishing achievement for an eighteen-year-old to reach the Olympic final.

And then, midway through the afternoon, a package came for him. It was sent by Team GB and it contained all the items he had left behind when he ran away from the stadium. In particular, it contained his phone and, with it, over a hundred texts from friends and teammates.

The message from everyone was the same. 'Be proud!' Everyone said it. Deon, Max, Spike. Everyone he cared about.

Danny liked that. He liked that a lot. He read and reread them.

Eventually, he was forced to emerge briefly from his room. He had no choice, his mother told him. And late that night, there was a knock at the door. Ricky came to tell him that someone had come to see him and he insisted on seeing him and he would not go away until he had spoken to him. It was Charles Perryman.

When Danny got downstairs, Perryman was

sitting in the living room with a cup of tea in his hand, chatting to his father. His father quickly exited the room, leaving Danny and Perryman together on their own.

'How are you, Danny?' Perryman asked.

'Pretty low,' Danny replied. 'About as low as I've ever been.'

'OK, Danny, I understand. But you've got to stop feeling sorry for yourself now. You can't just run away like this. I didn't pick you for the team so you could disappear the minute something went wrong.'

'I'm sorry, Mr Perryman,' Danny said. 'I didn't mean to let you down. I didn't want to let anyone down. But my Olympics are over.'

'No, they're not, Danny. They most definitely are not over. We need you back.'

'I don't understand, Mr Perryman. My Olympics are gone.'

'No, Danny. We need you in the relay team. You joined the ranks so fast that I never thought of using you in the relay. You've never practised with the team. It seemed too much of a risk. But we've just had an injury. One of the boys is down. We need you, Danny. We have a chance of a medal, a good chance. But without you we've got no chance at all. What do you think?'

Danny sighed. He felt emotionally drained, exhausted, finished. But how could he possibly say no?

'OK, Mr Perryman,' he said. 'I'm in. And I swear to you that this time I will not let you down.'

And, somewhere within him, Danny suddenly became aware that actually he wanted to run again.

★ 29 ★

ONE LAST CHANCE

When he stormed out of the Olympic Park on Sunday night, Danny had no intention of coming back. None whatsoever. But on Tuesday evening he moved back into Flat 32; on Wednesday he started practising with the relay team; on Friday they came second in their heat to Usain Bolt and the Jamaicans; and on Saturday evening they were in the Olympic final.

The sprint relay is a four-man team race. Team GB would have Deon Francis running the first leg; he would hand over the baton to Tyrone Small, who had run in the 200 metres; Small would hand over to Max Donne; and then Max would hand over to Danny.

The strong favourites were the Jamaicans: Usain Bolt plus three other speed machines. Second favourites were South Africa, and behind them the United States and Great Britain.

An hour before the race, the British team practised together on the warm-up track. It felt funny for

Danny to be there. He had to stop his mind from wandering back to the last time. But that wasn't too hard. He liked being in a team. He liked Deon and the boys. And they were now looking after him like a kid brother. They especially looked out for van Zyl. They wanted to protect Danny from him; everyone knew he was a bully. Not only did they want to win themselves a medal, but they particularly wanted to beat van Zyl and the South Africans.

There was one man who Danny had not seen much of since the previous Sunday – Spike, the man who Danny truly believed was the best coach in the world. Spike loved speed and he loved Danny, but he hated the relay. It was running in the relay that ended his own career and he always found the relays hard to watch. So Danny was surprised when Spike came and joined them at the warm-up track.

'Didn't think I would see you here, Spike,' Danny said.

'I know, I know,' Spike replied. 'It wasn't easy. But I had to come. I'm sorry I haven't brought the chess-board, but I had to see you.' They moved away from the rest of the team and sat on the side of the track together. 'I just wanted to tell you, Dan, that today is the first time I will have watched a relay live since my own career ended. I cannot stand them. But, much as I cannot stand them, I'm more desperate to see you run in one. In the Olympic final. You deserve a medal, Speedboy. Have you brought your speed today, Speedboy?'

'I think so, Spike.'

'Good. Because you'll need it. You'll need nothing else. Because you're ready. Today is your day. I want you to know that. Van Zyl has been so busy boasting these last few days he thinks he's better than he really is. I don't think he'll have a chance of matching you today. Today is your day, Dan. I'll be in the stands and so will your parents, your brother Ricky, and your friends, and so will thousands of people who so want you to do well. But don't think about us. Just think of Uncle Carl and Uncle Jesse. And then you'll be fine. Good luck, Speedboy.'

Danny watched as Spike got up and walked away. His limp seemed more exaggerated today. Maybe that was because it was relay day.

Before they went into the stadium, Deon gathered the four of them together in a huddle. Deon had turned himself into the team captain and he was good at it. Danny respected him. Deon seemed strong, reliable and not the sort of guy to be disqualified by a false start.

'Listen, boys,' Deon said, 'when we go into that stadium in a minute, it'll be for the very last time. Our last chance. The end of our Olympics. The end of the London Olympics. This is it. So don't leave any energy in your legs. I want to see it all out there on the track. Come on, boys! This is our chance! Our last chance. Let's make this the race of our lives!'

And, with that, they marched purposefully to the stadium. Suddenly, Danny felt good and confident. He recognized that feeling – the feeling of warmth running like a warm tap through his veins. He didn't feel nervous, not like the last time he was in here, not at all. *I've got it back*, he thought to himself. *I've got it!*

The team then separated and walked to their appointed positions around the track. Danny went to the place of the third handover and he smiled when he realized who he would be up against: not only Usain Bolt but Ryan van Zyl.

Good. Danny felt ready now. Van Zyl was just the last of his doubters. His schoolmates, his dad, the media – they'd all doubted his ability. And van Zyl was the last in the queue. *Good.* Danny felt strong. He felt it was time, at last, to prove the remaining doubters wrong.

He went straight over to Bolt and shook his hand. 'It's good to see you back,' Bolt said. Danny liked that.

There were no such pleasantries with van Zyl. The South African smiled his gold-glinted, toothy grin at Danny as he walked over. But Danny was ready for him this time. 'Hey, little boy,' van Zyl snarled, 'I thought you were too scared to run in the Olympics.'

'Well, you thought wrong,' Danny replied. 'But the main reason I came back was because I was looking forward so much to kicking your butt.' And for the first time since Danny had met him, van Zyl said nothing back. Nothing at all.

The runners lined up in their lanes and waited. Danny watched Deon in the blocks. He felt his heart beating, but he felt that reassuring warmth too. *Uncle Carl and Uncle Jesse*, he said to himself. *Uncle Carl and Uncle Jesse.*

Bang!

The gun went off and Deon did too; he got a good start, a great start. As he approached Tyrone, he was behind the Jamaicans, nearly level with the South Africans and ahead of the rest of the field.

Deon passed the baton to Tyrone and the hand-over was clean. Tyrone took off like a bullet down the back straight, but could make no headway against the Jamaicans or the South Africans. Great Britain were third, clearly third. *Come on, Tyrone! Come on, Tyrone!*

Tyrone handed over to Max and suddenly Great Britain were second. The Jamaicans were no longer running. They had dropped the baton; they were out of the race! *Come on, Max, we're second! Come on, Max!*

When Max approached Danny, there were two races going on and the Jamaicans were in neither of them. The first race was between South Africa and

Great Britain for the gold medal. The second was between the rest of the field as they battled it out for bronze. It was Danny against van Zyl for gold. The crowd was deafening, but Danny couldn't hear it; he could only concentrate on Max. He felt more focused and more ready than he had ever felt in his entire running life.

Danny felt that flush of warmth for the last time as Max thrust the baton into his hand. Van Zyl was half a metre ahead of Danny as Danny set off, powering his way down the finishing straight. *Pump it, Dan, high legs, pump*

20 metres gone and Danny was not cutting into van Zyl's lead.

30 metres: he could still get no closer to van Zyl. *Come on, Dan, keep your rhythm, pump and keep your rhythm.*

50 metres: still the small gap remained.

60 metres: was van Zyl tiring? Danny felt he was edging closer.

70 metres: he was almost on van Zyl's shoulder. Ahead of them on the big stadium screen, they could both see the gap closing. Van Zyl seemed to respond and get stronger, but Danny kicked again.

80 metres: *keep strong, Danny. Pump it, maintain rhythm.* Suddenly, they were side by side. Danny felt stronger, stronger than ever.

90 metres: van Zyl looked across to Danny. Big mistake. Never look, everyone knows that, because it will only slow you down. Never look. But the

expression on van Zyl's face said it all: he looked scared. Danny did not see this; he only had eyes for the line. He stretched forward his shoulders and dipped for it.

100 metres: he was the Olympic champion. He and Deon and Tyrone and Max. And he only knew this because, within seconds, the other three had joined him at the finish and were jumping all over him.

'Champions! Olympic champions!' Deon shouted. 'Danny, you made us Olympic champions!'

★ 30 ★
THE END

What do you do when your dream has just come true? What do you do when you have just won the Olympics?

The answer is you get your medal.

But first you have to talk to the people from BBC TV, and then the people from BBC radio, and then you have to talk to people from TV stations in America and Australia and China and Japan and, it seemed, pretty much every country in the world that Danny had heard of.

They all wanted to ask so many questions. 'Is it true you're still at school?' 'Is it true you live near here?' 'Is your father really a postman?' 'Do you think you'll beat Usain Bolt one day?' 'When will you beat Usain Bolt?' 'Are you going to be a postman one day too?'

Some of the questions were funny. Some were just silly. But Danny didn't mind. His dream had come true. All he wanted now was his medal.

He hugged Deon and then he hugged Max and

Tyrone. He wanted to hug his mum and dad and Ricky, and Spike too. He wanted to share this moment with them. But when you have won the Olympics, he discovered, you cannot do what you want. Olympic champions do what they are told.

All he wanted was a medal. And to show it to his family. But, after talking to all the TV reporters, he was told he had to go into a press conference to talk to more journalists.

The press conference room was under the Olympic Stadium and it was huge. It was bigger than the school hall at Newham Secondary. There was an army of cameramen at the back, and every seat in front of them was filled. There must have been about 250 people in there. *Who are they all?* Danny wondered. He felt slightly shy, slightly nervous. He recognized Pete O'Byrne, the guy from *The Times*, who had said he was too young to do well at the Olympics, Jenny Nicholas, from the *Daily Express*, who had also said he was too young. But no one else.

They started asking questions and Danny and his teammates tried to answer them.

A guy with an American accent asked: 'Is this the best day of your life?' Danny looked at Deon, Tyrone and Max and they laughed and then, exactly at the same time, they all said, 'Yes!'

And then they were asked about whether they felt proud, and they all said yes.

The next question was from Jenny Nicholas. 'Now

you've won your Olympic gold, Danny, at the age of eighteen,' she said, 'is there anyone in the world who can beat you in four years' time at the next Olympics?'

'I don't know,' he answered, 'it's impossible to say. I don't know if Usain will still be competing then.' And then he stopped and thought for a minute and came up with a much better answer. 'But there is one guy who I've raced many times and never beaten.'

'Who is that?' asked Jenny Nicholas.

'My brother. His name's Ricky. In my world, he's always been the fastest guy I know.'

The journalists went quiet momentarily and, when they could see that Danny was serious, they all scribbled fast into their notebooks.

And then, just when everyone was quiet, Danny leaned forward: 'Do you think I could ask you guys a question?'

The audience all nodded. They smiled. They seemed surprised. 'OK, thanks,' Danny said. 'When can I get my medal?'

This triggered laughter all around the room. Danny liked that, but he wanted an answer too. Eventually, Jenny Nicholas, who had been giggling loudly, told him: 'You're due up in thirty minutes!'

Half an hour later, Danny, Deon, Max and Tyrone stood waiting. The Americans, who won bronze, chatted to them happily. But the South Africans kept their distance and Danny chuckled to himself because, whenever he looked at van Zyl, the South African would look away.

There was an announcement inside the stadium: '100-metres relay, men, medal ceremony.' This was followed by a trumpet blast and then the South Africans, followed by the Britons and the Americans, were led through to the medal podium in the stadium where the crowds screamed their applause.

Danny looked around. He so wanted to see his parents and Ricky. But all he could see were 80,000 people clapping.

They were told to stand up on the podium and, at this stage, Danny could feel his heart beating fast. He had Max on his left and Deon on his right and all four of them put their arms round each other's shoulders.

They applauded as the Americans were given their bronze medals. They applauded again when the South Africans got theirs – but not quite so heartily. And finally, it was their turn. First Max, then Danny, then Deon and then Tyrone. The medal felt nice and heavy. Danny looked at it; it seemed the most beautiful thing he had seen in all his life.

'How many more of these are you going to get, Dan?' Deon said jokingly, as they stood to attention for the national anthem.

Danny felt proud; he felt amazing. He watched

the Union Jack flag being raised on the flagpole for gold medal-winners, and he sang loudly as 'God Save the Queen' was played.

He looked round the stadium and there, clearly, fifty metres to his right, he spotted them. His mum, his dad, Ricky. Only now did he feel tears welling up in his eyes. His Olympic dream had come true.

100-METRE FINAL STATISTICS

HISTORY OF THE WORLD
100-METRES RECORD

10.6 – Don Lippincott (USA) – 6 July 1912

10.4 – Charlie Paddock (USA) – 23 April 1921

10.3 – Percy Williams (Canada) – 9 August 1930

10.2 – Jesse Owens (USA) – 20 June 1936

10.1 – Willie Williams (USA) – 3 August 1956

10.0 – Armin Hary (West Germany) – 21 June 1960

9.95 – Jim Hines (USA) – 14 October 1968

9.93 – Calvin Smith (USA) – 3 July 1983

9.92 – Carl Lewis (USA) – 24 September 1988

9.90 – Leroy Burrell (USA) – 14 June 1991

9.86 – Carl Lewis (USA) – 25 August 1991

9.85 – Leroy Burrell (USA) – 6 July 1994

9.84 – Donovan Bailey (Canada) – 27 July 1996

9.79 – Maurice Greene (USA) – 16 June 1999

9.77 – Asafa Powell (Jamaica) – 14 June 2005

9.74 – Asafa Powell (Jamaica) – 9 September 2007

9.72 – Usain Bolt (Jamaica) – 31 May 2008

9.69 – Usain Bolt (Jamaica) – 16 August 2008

9.58 – Usain Bolt (Jamaica) – 16 August 2009

Ben Johnson (Canada) broke the world record twice. He improved it from 9.93 seconds to 9.83 in August 1987, and he set it even lower in the Olympic final in 1988 when he ran 9.79. However, both records were wiped from the record books when it was later discovered that he had been cheating by using drugs to help him run faster.

Tim Montgomery (USA) lowered the world record from 9.79 seconds to 9.78 on 14 September 2002. However, his time was also wiped from the record books when it was later discovered that he too had been cheating by using drugs to help him run faster.

The times in the list become more precise from Jim Hines's record in 1968 because that was when electronic timing was introduced. Before then, world records were all timed by stopwatch.

Usain Bolt's average speed when he broke the world record in Berlin in 2009 was 23.49 mph.

The fastest land animals are:

- Cheetah: 70 mph
- Pronghorn antelope: 61 mph
- Lion: 50 mph
- Wildebeest: 50 mph
- Thomson's gazelle: 50 mph

However, even these do not compare well with the fastest bird, the peregrine falcon, at 200 mph, or even the fastest fish, the swordfish, at 68 mph.

THE OLYMPIC 100-METRES WINNERS

1896 ATHENS OLYMPICS
Thomas Burke (USA) won in 12.0 seconds. This was the first 100-metre final in the modern Olympics.

1900 PARIS OLYMPICS
Frank Jarvis (USA) won in 11.0 seconds. He won when the favourite, Arthur Duffey, strained a tendon in the final.

1904 ST LOUIS OLYMPICS
Charles 'Archie' Hahn (USA) won in 11.0 seconds. Hahn was known as 'the Milwaukee Meteor'.

1906 ATHENS OLYMPICS
Charles 'Archie' Hahn (USA) won in 11.2 seconds. Hahn later wrote a book called *How to Sprint*.

1908 LONDON OLYMPICS

Reginald Walker (South Africa) won in 10.8 seconds. Walker was a nineteen-year-old clerk from Durban. He was coached by Sam Mussabini, who also coached Harold Abrahams, the 1924 winner.

1912 STOCKHOLM OLYMPICS

Ralph Craig (USA) won in 10.8 seconds. Craig would return in 1948, the next time the Olympics were held in London, as a member of the American sailing team.

1920 ANTWERP OLYMPICS

Charles Paddock (USA) won in 10.8 seconds. Before the final, Paddock was given a glass of sherry and a raw egg by his coach, supposedly to help him go faster. He died in a plane crash in the Second World War.

1924 PARIS OLYMPICS

Harold Abrahams (GB) won in 10.6 seconds. Arthur Porritt, the New Zealander who came third, later became the official surgeon of the British royal family.

1928 AMSTERDAM OLYMPICS

Percy Williams (Canada) won in 10.8 seconds. When Williams got back home to Canada, he was given a sports car as a reward for his achievement.

1932 LOS ANGELES OLYMPICS

Thomas 'Eddie' Tolan (USA) won in 10.38 seconds. One of the runners in Heat Two of this event was Liu Changchun, who was the first Chinese athlete ever to compete in the Games.

1936 BERLIN OLYMPICS

Jesse Owens won in 10.3 seconds. After becoming famous at the Olympics, to try to make some money, Owens ran in public races against horses, dogs and motorbikes.

1948 LONDON OLYMPICS

W. Harrison Dillard (USA) won in 10.3 seconds. Dillard's hero was Owens. He met Owens once, and Owens gave him his first pair of running shoes.

1952 HELSINKI OLYMPICS

Lindy Remigino (USA) won in 10.4 seconds. This race was so close that Remigino, convinced that he had been beaten, congratulated Herbert McKenley for winning. When he was told the actual result, he was astonished.

1956 MELBOURNE OLYMPICS

Bobby Joe Morrow (USA) won in 10.5 seconds. The bronze medallist, Hector Hogan, was an Australian and he died of leukaemia four years later.

1960 ROME OLYMPICS
Armin Hary (West Germany) won in 10.2 seconds. Hary was the first German ever to win gold in an Olympic track event.

1964 TOKYO OLYMPICS
Robert Hayes (USA) won in 10.0 seconds. Hayes would later become a professional American footballer and played for nine years for the Dallas Cowboys.

1968 MEXICO CITY OLYMPICS
Jim Hines (USA) won in 9.95 seconds. Hines's medal was later stolen from his house by burglars. He then placed an ad in the local newspaper asking to have it back and it was returned to him in the post.

1972 MUNICH OLYMPICS
Valeriy Borzov (Russia) won in 10.14 seconds. Borzov nearly missed his quarter-final because he fell asleep inside the stadium. He only just made it to the start-line in time.

1976 MONTREAL OLYMPICS
Hasely Crawford (Trinidad) won in 10.06 seconds. Crawford was Trinidad's first Olympic champion and had six calypso songs written in his honour.

1980 MOSCOW OLYMPICS

Allan Wells (GB) won in 10.25 seconds. Wells was coached by his wife, Margot, who has also coached rugby players, including Danny Cipriani, Paul Sackey and James Haskell.

1984 LOS ANGELES OLYMPICS

Carl Lewis (USA) won in 9.99 seconds. This was Lewis's first gold medal. He would win four in Los Angeles and nine Olympic golds altogether.

1988 SEOUL OLYMPICS

Carl Lewis (USA) won in 9.92 seconds. A very famous race. Ben Johnson, the Canadian, actually won by a very long way, in 9.79 seconds, but he was later found to have taken drugs and so was stripped of his medal and Lewis was made the winner.

1992 BARCELONA OLYMPICS

Linford Christie (GB) won in 9.96 seconds. Christie was thirty-two years old, the oldest Olympic 100-metre winner ever.

1996 ATLANTA OLYMPICS

Donovan Bailey (Canada) won in 9.84 seconds. Linford Christie, by now thirty-six years old, was in the final to defend his title, but he was disqualified for false-starting. He was absolutely furious.

2000 SYDNEY OLYMPICS

Maurice Greene (USA) won in 9.87 seconds. The silver medallist was Ato Boldon of Trinidad, who was Greene's training partner.

2004 ATHENS OLYMPICS

Justin Gatlin (USA) won in 9.85 seconds. Gatlin would later try to follow other sprinters and play professional American football. However, he never made the grade.

2008 BEIJING OLYMPICS

Usain Bolt (Jamaica) won in 9.69 seconds. This was a world record, but it was particularly amazing because he slowed down in the last 20 metres and, when he crossed the line, he was almost dancing.

WANT MORE ACTION? MORE ADVENTURE? MORE ADRENALIN?

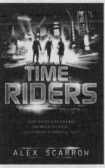

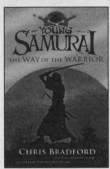

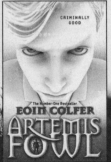

GET INTO PUFFIN'S ADVENTURE BOOKS FOR BOYS

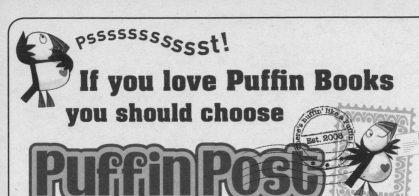

It all started with a Scarecrow.

Puffin is seventy years old.
Sounds ancient, doesn't it? But Puffin has never been
so lively. We're always on the lookout for the next big
idea, which is how it began all those years ago.

Penguin Books was a big idea from the mind of
a man called Allen Lane, who in 1935 invented
the quality paperback and changed the world.
**And from great Penguins, great Puffins grew,
changing the face of children's books forever.**

The first four Puffin Picture Books were hatched in 1940 and the
first Puffin story book featured a man with broomstick arms called
Worzel Gummidge. In 1967 Kaye Webb, Puffin Editor, started the
Puffin Club, promising to **'make children into readers'**.
She kept that promise and over 200,000 children became
devoted Puffineers through their quarterly instalments of
Puffin Post, which is now back for a new generation.

Many years from now, we hope you'll look back and
remember Puffin with a smile. **No matter what your age
or what you're into, there's a Puffin for everyone.**
The possibilities are endless, but one thing is for sure:
whether it's a picture book or a paperback, a sticker book
or a hardback, **if it's got that little Puffin
on it – it's bound to be good.**